A Fortnight in April

ISBN 978-1-7377945-2-3

Cover photography and design by the author.

This is a work of fiction. All characters in this work are inventions, and they do not represent real people, living or otherwise.

A Fortnight in April is a distant reference to John Reed's sadly enthusiastic Ten Days that Shook the World. The Peninsular Republic, though, is not a reference to Russia, old or new. There has never been a new Russia, for one thing, just the same old borscht, century after century.

This book is for Linda and Kerry, and for all the women in power, all over the world, doing a better job than a man would.

Cover illustration and design by the author.

Contents

Preface: Ad Proximum Vallem

There exists in the collection of human problems the idea that the well-being of the group is always in conflict with the freedom of the individual. That's nothing new. Over and over again, human thought and human action have slammed up against that wall. One can stay in one place and obey the customs of the group, or one can pack up, move to the next valley, and start one's own tribe. Obviously, that only works if the next valley is unoccupied or if you're prepared to subdue or eject its current occupants. And, even more obviously, it only works if there *is* a next valley.

Whether it worked or it didn't, that solution has been tried frequently by humans, and it's been advocated even more often. Fascism, anarchism, libertarianism, neo-capitalism — they all depend on what we can call *to the next valley* thinking. We can make it sound better by using a weak Latin version, *ad proximum vallem*, but it's the same old trap. You *will* run out of next valleys.

The fictional Peninsular Republic described in this and two of the author's previous books, appears as a political entity that tries to balance the interest of the whole and the one, and as any group made up of humans will always do, the Republic fails to achieve complete success at that. Its constitution recognizes the inevitability of that failure, and it specifically gives priority to freedom — referred to as Safety and Comfort — for the *group* over that of the *individual*. It accepts that there is no next valley, and it tries to make the current valley safe and comfortable for as much of the group as possible. This book and the others provide glimpses of how that might work out. If you were hoping for more sex and less irony, move to the next valley.

A Long Weekend

One thing to be said for climate change: the view from what had been Michigan Highway 22 — now PR 22 — had improved. Substantial parts of what had been Michigan and then the Peninsular Republic were now sunk in Lake Michigan. Also, people driving PR 22 north toward Elberta had more frequent views of the lake. In fact, what had been nearly level ground out west to the shore was now a set of low bluffs, overlooking a shallow bay. Immediately east of that new shoreline, some higher, deciduous-tree-friendly terrain had held up its hand, metaphorically, and said, "You shall not pass!"

The lake thought about that and eventually said, "Oh, okay. Fine." The village of Elberta itself was an easier target, anyway. The high water mark up there moved into the most westerly neighborhood, took a look around, and decided to stay. Back south, though, the lake left that new set of bluffs, close enough that what had been a couple of old roadside businesses were now lake-view properties. Highway 22 had been heading due west right about there, but long before, it had been sensible enough to turn north, and just after it did that, it ran by a small hotel and an equally small charging station/grocery/souvenir place.

If you pulled off the road into those businesses' joint parking lot, you'd be looking at their front walls, and except for names, they were essentially unchanged from their original states. The hotel had been built in the 1930s, just as Prohibition ended, and the owner built it with the proceeds from a speakeasy he'd been running in a cattle barn. The store came later, in the fifties, to serve the growing self-propelled vacationer market. Both places had been up and down, on and off since then, changing owners and business plans with the changes in tourism. When the Republic severed ties with the US, much of the old-line small-commercial segment packed up and left, angry at a new government that actually had their interests in mind. *Try to help me, will you?! Commie bastards!*

The Republic had done enough homework that it anticipated losing a segment of its small business owners, and it carefully preserved the better-kept assets, waiting for a new "Good old Fred, the shopkeeper" population to emerge. Not surprisingly, it did. But neither of these two highway-side businesses came into the hands of locals. Instead, after the Separation had sorted itself out, they were picked up by a pair of people tired of education, economics, technology, and cities. The hotel went to a technical guy in his late middle years, and the shop was picked up by a woman about the same age, with some retail experience and a desire to be out in the country.

The man's name was George Pickett—"no relation"—as he used to say. The hotel was in functional shape throughout, from its tiny complement of guest rooms upstairs to a first-floor dining room and bar and an up-to-code commercial kitchen. Pickett could have opened quickly, gated only by establishing supplier accounts and hiring a small staff. Looking at the physical plant, though, he decided to invest in at least one improvement first. The aggressive lake had given him a gift; by submerging most of the land to the west, it gave him seasonal entertainment. He punched through the opaque first-floor back wall and replaced it with weatherproof windows, gaining a free, ongoing meteorological floor show. He renamed the establishment "Sunset House."

Ciela Sarmiento, on the other hand, was less interested in providing an aesthetic experience and more concerned with serving as many customers as possible with the smallest amount of staff. The store had one apartment upstairs, and she intended to occupy it herself. The rest of the second floor was taken up with inventory space, and so was the basement. The first level was all customer-facing display and checkout counter. The electrical charge service outside was essentially hands-free. People pulled up, plugged in, inserted a card, and waited. Some of them came inside for purchases or a beverage. Others came for vacation-rental kitchen supplies, toys for children or dogs, minor repair products — duct tape was always a good seller — or entertainment. She had local information, paper copies of the national newspaper, printed magazines, and two racks of "local" books. One of the reasons people came up here from the cities was to escape "digitalis," as it was called: overexposure to electronic media. A large part of the printed material Ciela offered consisted of small paperbacks about the lakes, its storms, its people, and its shipwrecks.

All of that, with the exception of the supply of electrons from the chargers, was received, inventoried, deployed, and sold by Ciela herself or by one of her two employees. More accurately, she had two employee *positions*, cyclically filled by young people from the area. Working for the store wasn't going to be any kind of a launch pad, and kids signed up mostly to pull together a few Peninsular Republic Dollars—PRD, as the currency was known—before going off to some kind of educational experience.

Depending on the time of year, running the store—which she renamed "The Bluffs Shop"—was demanding; in her words, it was "a lot of work," seven months a year. For the remaining five, it wound down to something less than that. And since George showed up as the new owner of the hotel during one of those downtimes, she donated some of her energy to helping him with the preparation.

George had been born in Michigan, and Ciela came there with her parents from Cebu, in the Philippines. They arrived just in time to witness the Separation. Her mother didn't really want to experience more political instability ("We came here to get away from revolutions!"), but they stayed, got Ciela into the PR's new educational system, and "Here I am," she said, sitting at George's bar a few days before his opening, "Good luck," and they clicked their glasses together. Outside, a dog barked loudly.

===

"Damn it, just when you think you have a good, reliable enemy, they turn on you." General Alexiana Newhouse seemed tired. For someone at the head of a small nation's armed forces, reasonably positive approaches from its single biggest antagonist were more concerning than threats and bluster. "I mean, okay, fine. They ousted most of their right-wing leadership, they're cutting defense spending, they actually jailed a few politicians ... but what are they up to?"

She was speaking to a group of people who were concerned, professionally, with that question. Today, not far from thirty years after leaving the Union, the leadership of the only US State ever successfully to exit from the United States spent a substantial amount of effort puzzling out the puzzle that began at their southern border.

The meeting was partly in person and partly remote. A gentleman who was "dialed in" (as the quaint term still went) was of somewhat indeterminate age, not very tall, with a kind of old-school-academic affect. He smiled. "What worries me is this business of having *women* in control of things. What were they thinking?"

Newhouse grinned. "A woman President upset a lot of people down there. And not just men, either."

"I know. Even in their Congress, there seem to be some women who are terrified of women." His name was O'Neill, Otto O'Neill. Somewhere in some obscure or classified document, he must have had a title and job description, but no one seemed to know what it was. He was just one of those quietly indispensable figures, a power so far behind the throne as to be nearly invisible. And since the Republic had no throne at all, hiding behind it was very, very difficult. But he seemed to do it; he was known only to a few highly placed people in the government ... and one or two highly useful people without exalted places.

There were two others in the discussion, one in person and one more joining remotely. The second man on screen was the head of the national police service, the Security Branch, usually just called "SB." General Phillip Hallstatt was calling in from one of the nation's eight numbered Divisions; he was travelling around among them, interviewing people in his organization who held the rank of Major. The one unnumbered Division, the small square area surrounding the Capital, had just lost its commanding officer to a health issue. She was alive, but she and her partner were going to be absorbed in maintaining that state. Consequently, Hallstatt needed to identify a Major who was both ready for promotion and not critically needed in his or her current post.

The other person, the one actually present, was Hallstatt's peer in the more military piece of the Army, Field Branch or "FB". Her name was Sekhmet Kydo, and she was an extremely serious individual. She'd been tapped to run FB while its previous commander was out ill. He didn't survive his encounter with age, and Kydo had been given the permanent position, just as everyone assumed she would. She took sangfroid to extremes, but her staff and the eight Divisions she led were glad to have her in charge. "I don't envy you, General," she said.
"It gets worse," said Newhouse. "Phil, will you give us the new little issue?"

"Right. So, status quo, we need a new commander in Capital Division. We've got the First Brigade Major,

Kléber, standing in, but she doesn't want the job, permanently. And she's good; we need her where she is, and I'm not gonna order her to take the Division post. Still, as of right now, she's got the Division and First Brigade to look after. Lots of admin, lots of personnel stuff, plus, you know, actually keeping the peace. And just yesterday afternoon, the other Major ... the Second Brigade command, Wexler ... turned in his retirement papers. His partner wants to revive the family farm, I guess. Way up in Fifth Division. So ... we've got challenges."

"Is there someone in Fifth?" asked Kydo.

"Well, without getting too far into, um, confidential personnel things, no. Your group up there..." He meant the Field Branch Fifth Division. "... have serious stuff to look after. Water border with our pals in Canada, ice breaking, search and rescue. And they're on top of it. *Our* Fifth Div is not really ... that sophisticated.

"Oh," Kydo said.

"So," Hallstatt went on, "General Newhouse and I have a proposal. Not short term. Long term. And it's aimed at another problem, too. Maybe a two-birds thing."

O'Neill looked up. "Are we talking about the issue from yesterday, General?" He was addressing Newhouse.

"Yes, we are. In its simplest ... guise, whatever that means ... intel is broken, everywhere except here in Capital SB."

"I wondered if we might be getting to that."

"Yup. Phil and I cooked this up, and Kydo saw it just before we got together for this joyous little talk." The screen behind her desk woke up and displayed a list of issues.

- *SB intel groups in Divisions outside Capital are inefficient*
- *Tactically rather than strategically focused*
- *Intel supplied to Divisions 1-8 by Capital Div is inconsistently used*
- *24 Corporal or Sergeant positions across all 1-8 Divs dedicated to intel*
- *Average only 2.4 slots per Div filled*

"That's the set of causes. In essence, the Divisions aren't implementing local intel. Summary effects are:"

- *Missed opportunities within Div enforcement and prevention*
- *Wasted personnel effort and cost*
- *Consequences of failing to act on intel*

"And I don't have to preach to this choir." She waved a hand at the others. "We need to know more than we do, nationally for sure, maybe locally. We may have been optimistic about how well the Divisions could use intel for local issues. And for international info ... well, that's pretty much a Capital thing. Not all that local, really. So ..."

Proposed: reassign a subset of Divisional intel to Capital; return others to enforcement and prevention

Raise Capital intel to Brigade status
Promote current Capital intel personnel accordingly

"I see," O'Neill said. "So Capital becomes a three-brigade Division?"

"Yes, and there's a positive there, on the side." Hallstatt pointed at the last bullet. "By *promote personnel*, we mean moving Captain Gorsky up a notch to Major. That frees up Kléber from one thing, anyway, and the new Colonel will start out with a direct line to the Intel group."

"Ah. Yes, that does seem to be a good idea. Do we know how our friend Gorsky feels about it?"

"Not yet, no," said Newhouse. "We wanted to talk to you first ... you've worked with her, frankly more than I have."

Hallstatt nodded. "That, plus, unfortunately, the day before the Second Brigade Major gave notice, she and her partner went on a long weekend leave."

He's getting better, O'Neill thought. *He's managed to cut back on the commas and ellipses, except when he's talking off the cuff. Progress.* Aloud, he said, "Sadly, I, too am out of the office."

===

"It's been a while," said Kristin Horstel, looking out the window. "I mean since I could look at a big lake without giving a damn about the local school administration." Her view, in fact, was only a small lake, inland from the big one off to the west. There were two dogs, running along a small stretch of beach. Captain Eden Gorsky came up behind her and administered a hug.

"You've seen bigger ones."

"Don't remind me, darling. They all look alike, anyway." Kristin's career involved administering the administrators of the Republic's educational system. Three decades, give or take, of constitutional socialism had weeded out and early-retired the most incondite of the old guard, but there were still people who believed they knew better. The educational system was sternly focused on rearing a next generation of principled humans, signed up to the country's focus on safety and comfort for all, as opposed to anything that might come at the expense of *most* people for the benefit of a *few*. The ingenuity with which people couldn't keep that in mind was surprising. Kristin's job involved correcting them, at least if they had anything to do with education.

She was good at that. Since she and Gorsky had become partners, and since they'd found themselves moved down from the north woods to the Capital of the Republic, Kristin had become more and more involved in a renewal project for the Republic's national curriculum—the things it believed children needed to know. She managed, despite the demands of the work and the departmental complexities, to retain a capacity for deep affection, all of which she directed at her partner. She had a broad, middle-American face, moderately brown hair, and subtly blue eyes.

Gorsky, who disliked her given name, went by "E" when it was up to her. Over the last eighteen months, a dozen clever young people had become required to refer to her as "Sir" or "Captain." Although the Republic's general principle was to avoid typing people, the military and police elected to stick with *Sir*, no matter who was being addressed; no one wanted to make up something else, and none of the women in the service wanted to be called "Ma'am". So, Sir it was, regardless of physical or expressed gender.

Other than that, and as a matter of constitutionally mandated behavior, the whole society was required to be gender blind in anything but the most personal relationships. No one was a "husband" or "wife." If you were in an officially recorded relationship, you were a "partner." And since the formality of recording a relationship was exclusively related to joint finances, possessions, and responsibility for any children who might be hanging around, many people didn't bother with it. E remembered being introduced to an official who then introduced the person with her as "the man I'm currently sleeping with." To his credit, he neither blushed nor frowned, just said, "That's *with whom*, dear."

Today, E and Kristin would enjoy their first actual day of the vacation. Yesterday, they'd had 400 kilometers of train ride, then another 150 in a rented car. That investment of time brought them halfway up the spine of the Republic's Lower Peninsula to a town called Gaylord. From there, they drove themselves west in the car, toward the Lake Michigan shore and a rental house on a body of water called Crystal Lake. It wasn't actually

Lake Michigan, but it was just short of it: the big water was another 10 K to the west.

Both of them being used to running around the country, they brought along an evening meal, ate it, and relaxed. Now, with the trip and a night's sleep behind them, they were about to do some snooping around, picking out places to dine, and generally entering short-vacation mode. Kristin had been here once before, scolding the school district for deviationism, and she was poring over the binder of local information that the house owners supplied.

"I don't remember this one," she said, pointing out one of the menus. "It's right over on the lake shore." E looked at it.

"The Sunset House. Sure. And it says they "sometimes" have music."

===

The Sunset House, as a hotel, wasn't a massive enterprise. Of the rooms upstairs, four out of six were available for paying guests. George, the owner, occupied one of the other two himself. In the busy season, another one was reserved for live-in help: someone to clean up, change bedding, help with check-in and check-out, wrangle luggage. In the off season, Pickett handled those chores himself, with part-time assistance from a local family. When he needed somebody, he'd call, and whoever was on hand, not off at school, not wrapped up with child care and so on would drop in and make a few Peninsular Republic Dollars.

This morning, as the year was just waking up from winter, there weren't any guests at all. Since there was no one paying to eat breakfast, there was no real need to get up early and deal with it. George was still gathering himself up and considering menu choices for a limited lunch service and a less limited dinner. He'd deliberately assigned himself a back bedroom, since it gave him the same western view as from the dining room: Lake Michigan catching the first rays of sun coming over from the east side of the world.

Outside, the road was quiet. A truck rolled by, oddly silent. The final triumph of electric power had seen the death of the diesel, and few people regretted it. A minute or so later, a Security Branch patrol vehicle drove up from the other direction and turned in. As usual in the rural Divisions, there was a Corporal driving and a National Service trooper learning. After four levels of education — sixteen years of schooling at public expense — the Republic asked for a little payback. People newly given what the US would call an undergraduate degree got to give back two years of slightly-paid service in some part of the government. You could request a particular kind of work, and you might or might not get that specific thing. The young man in the SB car was doing his service in the Security Branch Sixth Division, and almost every working moment was instructional. This morning, his Corporal was introducing him to the business owners in their area, explaining how each one might be of help in investigating something or finding someone.

"This is Sunset House," she said, turning the power off. "There's the store, too, but we usually mean both places, when we drop in over here." She touched the communication screen and said, "Unit 623, out at Sunset House, routine." To her trooper, she said, "Routine means we got no issue here, just checkin' up. Showin' the flag, you know." The young man didn't, in fact, know that term, but he noted it. "Let's go see if George's up, introduce you, see if he's got any gossip for us."

As they got out of the vehicle, the lights came on in The Bluffs Shop. "That's Ciela's place. Snacks and Electricity, pretty much. We'll introduce you to her, too. Once in a while, she has a shoplifting thing." Instead of going to the front, they walked around to the back and tapped on a solid wood door. There was no immediate response, and the Corporal knocked again, then tried the door; it opened. She took one step in, then said, "Oh, there you are."

George was just coming through the double-swinging kitchen doors with a paper bag in his hand. "Help, police, burglars," he said in a conversational tone. He set the bag down. The Corporal introduced her new trooper and had a few words with George. He had nothing to report, essentially. Even traffic on the road was calm, at least at this hour.

"Well, good," she said. "May no new thing arise." She'd been born in Fourth Division, outside Grand Rapids, and she had an undergraduate degree in literature. After that, though, she did her National Service up here in the Sixth, and got a taste for it. Most of her rustic affect was a way of fitting in with the genuine locals. "We'll go say hello to Ciela, and then be on our way."

"Say hello," George said. Ciela was coming in the door behind them. There was just a moment of surprise on her face, but the familiar pattern of introducing the new kid explained the police presence. The same general exchange took place, the same "nothing to report" from her, and as the cops turned back to the door, George handed Ciela the bag he'd brought with him. She took it without comment and left, too, heading back to her place of business.

The cops got back in their car. "Okay," the Corporal said, "Got any thoughts about that?"

"Um, about what, exactly?"

"George has a bag of something, and he gives it to her. Nothing said. But we were there. Think that might mean something?"

"Oh ... something illegal?"

"It might be, but I've got another theory. She didn't really look like she'd ... fixed herself up, yet. Got ready to serve the public, you know? And she's coming across the parking lot, early in the morning, to get something in a bag from George." The trooper looked baffled. She went on. "I've kind of wondered about this for a while, with those two, and my guess is, that bag contained some intimate item of clothing she'd left behind. If you follow me." The young man opened his mouth, paused, and shut it again.

===

"So where you wanna meet this time? At the Tap? Or over at the Draft Horse?"

"The Tap's quieter. Over there, around seven?"
"Fine." The call ended; a man in his early thirties put away his phone. The balance on his credit card was growing, and he wasn't hearing a lot from his employer. The breakfast he'd just finished was self-prepared, eaten at a counter in his own rented apartment. Of the two meeting locations just discussed, the Draft Horse was right across the street in a small Indiana town. The selected meeting location was a mile and a half west, looking over a body of water called Hall's Lake. The "Tap" was the only actual business in the little cluster of houses along the east shore. From either his place or the chosen bar, the Peninsular Republic's border was just a couple of miles north.

===

In the Republic's Capital city, much of what had been a major public university had been converted into government space. The football stadium and its surroundings had been taken over as the national government complex. It had been roofed over and supplied with some environmental and physical protections. Now, it hosted a large percentage of the country's bureaucracy.

Next to it, a saucer-like performance venue had become the Council's meeting chamber. Designed for twelve thousand spectators, it housed in some comfort the eight hundred members of the national legislature and its staff. Referred to as "the Council," the people involved were the only elected officials in the country. In a kind of bloodless institutional purge, all governance had been centralized. Except for Council members, everyone involved in governing the Republic was a government employee, not a politician. And everyone, elected or not, was ultimately supervised, not by a human, but by the Constitution itself.

Until recently, the Security Branch Capital Division had been in another governmental outbuilding, close to the Council. In the last year, though, it had moved. Growing headcount and increasing concern with digital intelligence had driven a move to another building, a holdover from university administration, closer to the main campus itself. It offered four stories of very solidly built concrete, dating to the 1960s and reflecting a certain paranoia about student revolution. It looked like a cubist citadel.

Now, in this brave new world, the socialist state agency of coercion had moved in. On this particular mid-day, in a sort of courtyard, three young women, two of them wearing Security Branch uniforms and one a kind of mildly business-like outfit, were standing together and singing. And the tune wasn't 'The Internationale.'

One of them—the one in civilian attire—came in on the final line. "When she saw the burnin' o' Airlie..." she sang, drawing out the last word: "Airrrleee." They all smiled. "Eventually, I'll learn the rest of it," she said. A man in a Corporal's uniform walked up, and two out of three saluted.

"You're getting this down," he said. "What was that last one?"

"'The Bonnie House O'Airlie.' Archie Campbell and the Argyles coming to burn the house of a man who's off supporting King Charles against religious weirdos."

"That's a pity. But it sounded nice, anyway. Carry on."

"Yes, sir." All three of the singers were in the Capital Division Intelligence Company, the only one funded and commanded across two departments. Two of this trio were paid by Security Branch and the other by External Relations—a State Department by another name. That person was Meg Cordell, and she was coming to the end of her National Service. She and her two colleagues had discovered a mutual enthusiasm for folk music; in reasonable weather, they spent part of their lunch period out in the courtyard, singing and talking about it.

"I should go in," said one of the SB troopers. "I have to see if my script ran."

"Okay, Chris. We'll be there in a minute. Meg, I wanted to ask how your dinner went?"

"Oh ... it was ... fun, I guess. We hadn't seen each other in a while."

"So, not 'The Maid Gaed Tae the Mill By Necht,' exactly?"
Meg didn't actually blush, but it was close.
"No! Nothing like that."

"Oh. Too bad," said her friend.

===

As E and Kristin were getting ready for a scouting trip, looking for views and places to picnic, making a grocery list and noting shops to acquire the things on it, E's personal phone rang. "Oh ... dear."

"Trouble?"

"I hope not." She answered it. "Yes, General?"

It was Phil Hallstatt, He was very apologetic, quite sorry to interrupt her leave, no action required, just a heads up; the sort of introductory text that panics everyone when one of the bigger dogs calls.

E listened for about two minutes, then said, "Yes, sir. I see how that could be helpful ... to Major Kléber. And I'm certainly willing to support the changes ... Yes, completely." Pause. "Very well. Thank you for the heads up. I'll be back Monday. Goodbye."

Kristin looked her in the eye. "Trouble?"

"Well, no. Or ... sort of, I guess. Someone, somewhere, seems to think I know what I'm doing ... apparently."

"Really? You?"

"Yes. We've suddenly got two levels of command vacant. People leaving for medical reasons. Or just retiring. And someone thinks that calling my little group a brigade and promoting me will somehow help."

"Didn't you just *get* promoted?"

"Yes, but that was, what? a year and a half ago. So, Monday, when we're back and I go into the office, I'll get a red badge."

"A Major!?"

"Yes, and until we find a new Colonel, apparently I'm reporting right to General Hallstatt."

"Who the hell are you sleeping with, back there?"

"There's this person in the Department of Education. She has a lot of connections."

"Flatterer. Let's go buy some groceries. Before they make you Queen."

===

"One thing done, anyway." General Hallstatt ticked "Gorsky" off his list of people to talk to. He was, himself, a generally kind individual. Kindness was not, though, high on the requirements for the head of a national police agency, and that yielded a level of conflict. He was a gay man in command, in a society that didn't link gender with power. He had to be just an officer, period. His own area of comfort was *maintaining order*, but the random universe was pushing him beyond that, whispering that order didn't have a single definition or an unlimited life.

"The nature of order, Phil," it said, "is to change."

"Oh, all right. If you insist," he'd reply. Now, he went back to the personnel issues of the day, replacing a Colonel and a Major, simultaneously, in the country's geographically smallest but most strategically important Division.

===

Meg Cordell was not a large person. One and a half meters tall, plus a bit, and slim, she still gave the impression of being rooted wherever she was. She wore her dark hair in a helmet shape, coming down below her ear lobes and reaching down in front just to her equally dark eyebrows. Looking at her, you'd assume a northern European genome, accented with very dark brown eyes. She'd had reasons, earlier in her life, not to smile; now, though, she was finding more and more reasons to, and it was a contagious smile. She did, often, seem to be looking beyond you, looking for what might happen later, for what you might become, eventually.

She'd been raised in a defiantly religious home, without brothers or sisters, just a grim, disappointed set of parents, unhappy with the change in government and still part of a church. During Meg's first year of college, that church had crumbled in a pharmaceuticals smuggling scandal. Meg had just left school, unable to reconcile anything with anything, effectively. And then her parents had separated, with her mother leaving for the US and Meg left behind with her withdrawn and unloving father. She'd been fortunate to encounter an old high school acquaintance, and with his assistance, left home and moved into one of the government's "houses" for confused, unhappy young people.

Meg emerged from that and subsequently from college, no longer at all confused, and only, still, a bit unhappy. She'd signed up for her required two years of National Service, requesting and getting an internship with External Relations. Her assignment was with Captain Gorsky's Intelligence group, becoming one of several ER people working on the same kind of snooping and probing and analyzing as the military staff there. To her delight, she found that she was quite good at it.

===

The Hall's Lake Tap was located on the east shore of, not surprisingly, Hall's Lake. It was larger by perhaps a third than the surrounding houses, and it was the only commercial property nearby. It had plenty of parking — the road curved around it and ended in its parking lot — but no outdoor public space. Granted, the view from a front porch or a raised deck would have been limited to the houses, sheds, and garages across the street. *They* had backyard lake frontage, but the tavern was essentially an adult refuge from what was otherwise a very families-with-children community. The Tavern was where Dad and sometimes Mom would go to get a bit of peace. Friday nights, there would be "entertainment" — a sign said so — and after ten PM, whatever else that meant stood down, and a young woman, brought in by the bar owners from somewhere outside the community, would dance unclothed to juke box tunes. This had been going on so long that no one really paid much attention, either legally or in an aesthetic sense. It was just a thing that went on.

At the current moment, it was midday, and no one was dancing, clothed or not. Two men were at the bar, having beers and discussing some kind of fishing gear. Another one was talking to the bartender about boat repair. And at a table, two other gentlemen were planning armed insurrection. Quietly.

One of them, a local named Lou, was taking the case against, at least for the specific proposal the other one was suggesting. His objections were on tactical grounds, not philosophical principles. The other man, Rich, was arguing that the problems were solvable; to put it simply, it could work.

"I know," he said. "The highway's there. But that's good. It's an advantage. Once we're set up, north of there, we control it. And we can shut it down, again. You know, threaten to."

"Yeah, but what if ..." The conversation went on along those lines. The idea seemed to be, in essence, that if a group could close a large freeway for enough time to get an armed group across it, they could open it back up, but only if certain requirements were met. Presumably, those requirements had already been discussed.

"You know what we got there? That thing's an asset. We're up there, up north. Out of the country. But if they mess with us, we're close to something they depend on. Lots of companies, lots of people's income."

"You sayin' we charge ... what's it called, tolls?"

"Not at first. We're just sayin', leave us alone. Or else. Then later, maybe we up the price."

"Well, it sounds good. All I'm thinkin' about is the crossing, in the first place. We gotta get sixty or seventy people, thirty or so trucks across all that."
"Yeah. But just once. Then we're there. And we got our high card. There ain't another big interstate goin' east/west, clear down to Indianapolis. We do this, and we got I-80 and I-90 in the palm of our hand."

===

The day was winding down. E and Kristin had driven around for most of it, going up to Frankfort for supplies, making sandwiches in the car and eating them at a park. Sticking with PR22, they went on north along the isthmus between the big lake and Crystal Lake, stopping at the Point Macready Lighthouse (named to honor one of the few people actually injured in the Separation). Kristin took photos of the lighthouse itself, then the interface of lake and land, getting in close to shoot the small waves as they ran up a foot or so of beach, then died away.

E just looked. Some of what there was to see reminded her of her time in the Upper Peninsula, dealing with minor crimes in an isolated, four-person SB post. *Dog Island*, she thought. *Pre-Kristin. That's not a place I want to go, right now.* Depending on your definition, Kristin may or may not have been a first love, but she was the one that stuck, the one that took hold. She'd never said so, aloud, but E had a private commitment, articulated often — usually when some kind of organizational issue or law enforcement crisis arose: *the job is not more important than us.*

"So," Kristin said, "what now?"

"Do you want to try the Sunset House place? We could drive around Betsie Lake, just for the sun on the water, and by the time we got back around to Frankfort, it'd be more or less dinner time."

"Great. And we can find a hiking place, say, tomorrow."

"That's a plan."

===

George Pickett took breaks as often as possible, going out back and just looking at the lake. It was sparkling, now, as the sun declined. Once in a while, Ciela was able to get away and join him for one of these moments, but she had three customer vehicles in the parking lot and two on chargers. This was her season, just like his, to cut back on full time staff, and while that was good for the financial situation, it meant she worked either up to closing time or to the point when there was no longer anyone interested in electrons or beer. She and George were both relatively new members of the local business community — in comparison to others, anyway — and although they had many acquaintances, neither of them had close friends. *Another ten years,* George thought, *and maybe I'll actually know a few people.*

Tires on gravel got his attention. He glanced at the store's parking lot, but it hadn't turned in there. *Dinner guests*, he thought, and he went back inside.

Gorsky stopped the car. There was one other vehicle parked by the restaurant, a sedan. A man was unloading something from the trunk, and as he turned around, he had a guitar case in his hand. "Look," Kristin said, "must be the entertainment."

"Good. I mean, if it *is* good. I'm not really in a C and W kind of mood."

"Hmm. No. Me, either."

E started to open the door, then noticed a light on the dash. "You know," she said, "maybe I should take the car over there ..." she pointed at the store "... Get it charging while we eat."

"Fine. I'll get a table ... maybe not right next to the band. Just in case."

As E moved the vehicle, Kristin went inside. George raised a hand from behind the bar. "Welcome. Have a table, any table." She looked around. Off to the right, there was a piano. Someone was sitting at it, arranging scores. Another man was setting up a couple of sheet music stands.

"How about this one?" she asked, pointing to one in the middle of the room. As she looked around, though, she saw the back windows and their view.

"Or ... maybe back there?"

"Anywhere you like. I'll be right with you."

"Great." She walked over toward the lakeside tables, noticing that the man at the piano had gotten up. He was somewhere near or past fifty, at a guess, dressed as casually as his colleagues, clean-shaven and with only minimal hair remaining. None of that was unusual, but she was mildly surprised when he walked the two or so meters over to her, smiling. "Hello," she said.

"Hello. Please forgive me, but are you not a friend of Captain Gorsky? I think I may have seen you together at some sort of function. In the Capital, I mean."

"Now let's see ... the last thing we went to, *en suite*, would have been the new curriculum launch celebration. I'm in DOE."

"Yes, yes. I remember, now. A very pleasant evening."

"Are you in the government? I'm not sure we actually met."

"I have some minor advisory duties. I've had the pleasure of working with Captain Gorsky."

At that moment, Gorsky came in the door. She looked around, then stopped. *What?!* Her partner was sitting at a restaurant table, way the hell up in the north country, chatting with Otto O'Neill.

===

At the eastern border of Ohio, Interstate highway I-80 becomes the Ohio Turnpike. Under that name, it runs west across all of Ohio. Just west of the border with Indiana, I-80-and I-90 continue together, still as toll roads. Soon, they turn sharply north-west, heading on into Indiana. They cross I-69, running north/south near a place called Steerling, and then they turn back west. As toll roads, their entrances and exits remain few in number. As they follow the southern border with the Peninsular Republic, just half a kilometer south of it, the country around them becomes sparsely populated farmland. About 12 K later, they turn back south a bit. But in that whole near-border experience, there's no legitimate way on or off, and only five local roads run over or under the highway.

Most of the land, north or south of the highway, is cleared and farmed. But near the end of the westward run a nature preserve, following a small stream, makes a large patch of woods, and it extends from the northern edge of the toll road, right up into and beyond the US border. The woods take up a mostly unpopulated area on the eastern edge of the Army of the Republic's Second Division. The border is marked by a high chain-link fence, but since no roads cross the wooded area, there's no substantial defensive position. There's none at all, in fact, except for the fence.

===

As E and Kristin drove back to the house, the conversation was essentially a deconstruction of the fairly constrained talks with O'Neill. After a few pleasantries, he'd gone back to the piano. At a break, when he and his friends were being set up at a table, he'd come by again, and a few more studiedly mainstream things were discussed — restaurants, Kristin's work, and, obliquely, the empty positions in Capital Division. He always put himself in the role of observer, someone who was aware of events, but not one who influenced them. Nor did he talk in more than the most superficial way about E's group and its work.

"You know," E said to Kristin, "we've been down this path before ... that there are classified things. O'Neill is sort of classified, himself. I think. There are people with higher rank than mine who don't know him. Or if they do, they don't say. But every time something weird is going on — at least that I know of — he's in it. Working on it."

"Okay, but ... what's he doing up here, playing soft-pedal progressive jazz?"

"That's a really good question. If I'd thought of ... something he might do, on a vacation ... it might be with a house, somewhere, and a housekeeper to shop and say "O'Neill? Never heard of him." You know, if someone asked. I would *not* have imagined this."

"So ... do I tell anybody? Or not?"

"I think the best thing is not. Unless somebody else mentions it. You know, *O'Neill says he ran into you and Gorsky up north.* Something like that. Then, maybe, just say what happened. See if they say ... I don't know, more than that. Because, he saw you first. And connected us. And came over to say hello. On one level, that might be damage control. *I'll just act natural.* But I think it might be more *Oh, it's Gorsky's partner. Gorsky will know what to say and not to say. I'll go be sociable.* And the more I think about it ... what's the difference, really, seeing him here and seeing him at the DoE party? I didn't see him there, but he saw us."

"Well, this isn't really a den of ill repute, anyway. Not like we saw him, I don't know, in a US Embassy."

"Right. Right. That's ... yeah, why *not* run into him? Why shouldn't he do something he enjoys?"

"And speaking of which ... " She put her hand on E's thigh. There was a map display on the dashboard. Kristin nodded at it. "Twelve point three more kilometers."

===

Monday

Must ... not ... panic. It wasn't a usual train of thought. In a year, plus a bit, she'd managed quite well, not panicking. But in that time, she'd had little reason to; there hadn't been much success at anything else, but that was a different set of concerns. When she was new at this, poking around in Washington, she'd wondered how a job that sounded so simple could be so ... difficult. She thought about the early briefings from her manager, reviewing a list of departments to focus on, people to contact, things to find out, and the repeated suggestion that her physical appearance was an asset. "Don't hesitate to play that card," he'd said. "It's a fundamentally corrupt society. Play by their rules."

Right. Easy to say. But Katherine Connor—that was her actual name, as distinct from an assumed one—had discovered a different reality. Everyone who might be useful to approach was carefully "guarded" against fresh, new faces, just as they were guarded against violence. Every event she managed to get into was full of important males, each one accompanied by a dazzlingly attractive young female or a well-dressed, sophisticated, sober wife. So far, she'd only managed to sleep with three low-level, ill-informed men, plus one woman who was very nice, but wouldn't talk shop at all.

And then, the election turned everything upside down. Suddenly, half the city was looking for jobs, and the other half was trying to adjust, for only the second time in US history, to a woman President. Plus Secretary of

Defense. Plus Treasury. Connor was standing in her bedroom, looking at herself in a mirror. Again, as often before, the word "commodity" came to mind. But it couldn't take root in the anxiety area because there was no room.

Half an hour ago, there'd been a phone call, on what she called her "work phone" — a PR-spec secure device that she used only in private. No one but her contact, Doctor Wickham, had ever used it. But this time, it was someone else, and he'd had only three things to say. Wickham had been reassigned, and Connor would be getting a call from a new supervisor, shortly. And she was to do *nothing* until she received further instructions.

===

When Gorsky got into the office on Monday, she was still a bit tired. *Can't blame jet lag. Is there such a thing as train lag?* She had a Corporal as a kind of gatekeeper — no one said "Secretary," anymore, at least in the Army — and he showed her a list of messages and etcetera that had accumulated. None of it was dramatic. She assumed the drama would start up shortly, though. And with that thought, the person who was, at least officially, her immediate superior got off the elevator.

Lena Kléber was in full-time command of the First Brigade of the Capital Division. She was also standing in as the Colonel of the Division itself. And as of last week, she was acting in command of the now headless Second Brigade. She looked a bit stressed. "Welcome back, E," she said. "Let's just talk in your office. I haven't got time to get into classified stuff, quite yet."

In the office, she jumped right in. "So, Hallstatt briefed you, right? On the Third Brigade thing?"

"Yes. Friday morning."

"And you said yes, I hope?"

"I did. It made a kind of strange sense, and you look like you could use a little help."

"I've given up trying to hide it. Here's the absolute minimum we need to do, like, today." She took a small red square of canvas out of her shirt pocket. "So, pull that blue one off and put this on. And then sign this." She handed over a single sheet of military-speak. A glance showed Gorsky that the gist was as expected: *promoted to permanent rank of Major, agrees to uphold and support, etc., etc., Temporary reporting: General P. Hallstatt, Permanent reporting: Colonel, Capital Division SB, (position vacant).* A handwritten asterisk appeared at that point, and it referenced a note at the bottom of the page, * *Dual reporting responsibility, Doctor Jerilyn Klein, Assistant Director, External Affairs.*

"Sound like what you heard?"

"Yes. What about creating the Third Brigade?"

"All in here," Kléber said, handing over another document, this one apparently calling for twice as many pages. "All right?"

"I'll trust you," she said, and signed the last page. She pulled off her hook-and-loop blue badge and stuck the new one in place. It was only slightly crooked.

"Okay, then. I really only have one thing more that I can deal with right now, but it's kind of important. Who do you know who might want to run Second Brigade?"

"I hoped you'd ask that. After the General told me all the reasons, including that one, for that stuff ..." She indicated the paperwork she'd just signed. "... someone did come to mind. Morgan Matthews. Major, kind of without portfolio, up in Seventh."

"I don't get it? She's without a command?"

"The big reorg last summer? She was odd person out, up there. She'd be good. Do you want me to call her?"

"Sure. And ... you know, do it like this. Say we've got an open slot. See if she's willing to talk, at least. And if so, call me and I'll call her. Hallstatt has me fixed up to just yank people out of their chairs and bring 'em down here, if we want to talk. Get 'em on flights, the whole thing."

"Okay. First thing, I want to talk to the ... new Brigade ... so they're not hearing rumors. And Klein will probably be over here any minute. But I'll make that call in between. Let's see if we can get Second off your plate."

Kléber blinked a couple of times. "Thanks ... Gorsky. Thanks a lot. I gotta go."

===

"So over here, over west? About four miles? That's the first place to get off an' on the freeway. At that end. It's a toll booth. And just east of that's where we want to cut traffic off. Over there." The man talking was also pointing at places on a paper map. "Now, goin' the other way, it's a lot longer. Thirteen miles. But it's a big toll place."

One of the others said, "A toll plaza. Steerling."

"Right. And we don't wanna be close to towns and stuff. So back here ..." He pointed at the map " ... there's this maint'nance shop. "Big dome thing for salt, an' all that. And if we shut it down a little short of there, it's all just ... country. An' we got ten miles, almost. You know, to work with."

"What about all them little roads, runnin' up to it from the south?"

"That's what we're gonna use. We're gonna stage down here ..." He pointed at the map. "Big ol' farm, and the guy owns it, he's with us. We got these little roads here ... and here ... the highway's at level, ground level, you know ... and we just go down one ditch, across both lanes, down another one, and we're there. Quarter mile, straight north and into the trees."

"Are we over the border, there?"

"Two hundred fifty yards more, and we're over. We're back in the trees, and deployin'."

"What about the guys who blocked the highway?"

"As soon as we're across, we give 'em a call, an' they come join us."

"Well, hell. Sounds like we could do it. Rich did his homework, I guess." Another one spoke up.

"How many people do we want?'

"As many as we can get, right?"

"As many as we can fit in the trucks, anyway."

===

While Gorsky was working out what she'd tell the twenty-three people who constituted Third Brigade, Doctor Jerilyn Klein tapped on her still-open office door. "Good morning," she said. Klein was in her early seventies, but she didn't look like it. In fact, if you were guessing, you'd probably be off by a decade if not more. She was a long-standing asset within the Republic's External Relations Department, and half of Gorsky's new Brigade were ER people, assigned by Klein, employed and paid by ER. Up to now, the whole group, including Gorsky, had reported jointly to Klein and to Major Kléber.

"So...," Klein began, "We seem to have to come to a ... crossroads? ... in our relationship."

"Or something, anyway. What do you think about it? And did anyone think to ask your opinion?"

"They asked. And frankly, I don't see that it makes all that much difference. Nice new badge, by the way."

"Thank you. Sort of garish, but what the hell."

"I think we'd kind of reached parity, of a sort, already. When was the last time I gave you any straight-up orders? I ask for your opinion, and it usually matches mine."

"True. And we really do need to get some of the heat off Kléber. She was just here, and she didn't look happy."

"I know. And ... actually, we ought to go in the closed room. For some of the stuff I need to tell you."

"Sure. But can we get the team together, first? Change panics people. And I don't want a department full of people any more panicked than they usually are."

"Sure. Most of 'em haven't seen my smiling face for a while, anyway."

===

Back in his office, in what had been a university department building, Otto O'Neill was looking at a list of "things." That was the heading that his assistant used, and it was appropriate. The range of issues that came to O'Neill's attention was extremely diverse, with the only real commonality being urgency. Everything the government asked him to do or asked him about was, by definition, important. If not, they'd be asking someone else.

The list was not ranked, except by arrival. In data management terms, it was first in, first out, even if "out" only consisted of Otto passing it to someone else. Since he'd been gone for several days, there were more bulleted points — more "things" — to look over than usual. The first one read "International: Call Dr Green" followed by a phone number and a link to a government site.

The site in question was an extended and restricted personnel listing, allowing people with the appropriate permissions to see *who*, *what*, and *where* information on any individual in the government. In the case of Doctor Green, Otto knew him, but he still went out to the site, just to ensure that his memory was accurate. "Wallace Green, PhD, Vice Director of Research, Department of External Relations," he read. *As I remembered.* He called the number.

Instead of an assistant, Green himself picked up the call. "Mister O'Neill. Thank you for calling me. We have an issue over here, and I need your advice." O'Neill smiled. *It's so nice when people just get right down to it.*

"I'm happy to help. What seems to be the trouble?" Green told him what the trouble was. Five minutes later, the call ended. O'Neill looked over the brief notes he'd taken, then picked up the phone again. He called General Newhouse.

===

Gorsky's command was housed in a secure floor of its own, in the SB building. Offices and cubes ran around the periphery, and there was a large open space in the middle, partly as expansion room and partly for ad hoc, stand-up meetings. Now, there were eighteen people leaning on tables or standing, plus Gorsky herself and Klein. "Good morning," Gorsky began. "I've got some organizational news ... nothing too earth-shaking, but, at the very least, you'll see changes in personnel records and so on. So Doctor Klein and I wanted to give you the latest. Doctor?"

"Oh, you go ahead. There isn't all that much difference on the ER side."

"Okay. When we all came in this morning, we were a Company within the First Brigade, here. We reported to Major Kléber. About fifteen minutes ago, she came to see me, and about two minutes after that, we became Third Brigade, Capital SB Division, reporting to the Division Commander ... when we get one. Until then, I report to General Hallstatt." She paused, looking around at the audience. There were expressions of surprise, one or two confused looks, no apparent concern.

"As the more alert of you may have noticed, I have a different colored badge. Apparently, if you're in charge of a Brigade, you have to have one of these. However, I'm not going to let it go to my head. At least until I get used to this, bowing down in homage will not be required." Some laughter. Gorsky was not much of an authoritarian. As she kept reminding herself, she'd been a Sergeant just a single-digit number of years ago.

Klein smiled and said, "Those of you in ER will still have to bow to me, however."

Gorsky picked up on that. "All of this is essentially Security Branch stuff. We're still a joint group with External Relations. If you report there now, you still do. You will ... continue to ... I mean." She made a circular movement with her hand. "I'm really kind of winging it, here. I was still trying to grow up and be a Captain, and now ... " There was some laughter. "Anyway, that's what I had to say. And yes, I had a lovely vacation, thanks for asking." She turned to Klein. "Do you want to finish up in the closed ..." Klein's phone rang.

"Yes, doctor." There was a pause. "I see. We're just about to go back into a secure area. Major Gorsky and I will call you from there."

Gorsky cocked an eyebrow. "Issues?"

"Not sure. I said I'd call back from inside."

===

 As the staff of Third Brigade went back to their search algorithms and analytic scripts, the new structure was either interesting to them or not. The External Relations people were less interested, on average, than those in Security Branch. Some of the SB people, on the other hand, were now thinking about their current Company rank versus a similar position in a Brigade. The possibility of badge color upgrades for more people than just Gorsky was an interesting thought.

Meg Cordell, being in ER and — as a National Service intern — at the bottom of the rank structure there, didn't have much reaction at all. Her professional concerns were about producing the best results she could, hoping that it would help her transition to a full position in the group. Her two years' National Service was almost complete, and she wanted to stay in ER and continue with the team. On a personal level, the things on her mind were more tactical. Specifically, she had a lunch ... date? ... with an old acquaintance, and the question was really as simple as that. *Is it a date or not?* Either way, she'd be skipping today's folk singing.

===

In the secure conference room, Klein called an ER number. "Doctor Green," she said to Gorsky. "A colleague of my boss. Didn't sound happy."

The man in question answered his phone. "Confirm for me that you're in a closed area." Klein did, also noting that Gorsky was present. "Very well. The issue is this. Did you know Albert Wickham?"

"I met him once or twice."

"I won't go into the details, but the summary is that he requested and received headcount additions for two research staff. A little over a year ago. They were intended to be headquarters staff, under his direct supervision. An audit has just shown that two people were hired, but neither of them is here." He paused.

"Not at headquarters?"

"Not in the Republic."

The story that followed didn't reflect well on ER's personnel procedures. Wickham had been able to hire two people, a young man and a young woman, then get them forged US passports and into the US. One of them went to the Capital and appeared to have been trying to collect confidential information on economic issues. ER had been able to contact her and instruct her to stand down and stand by. The other one was not responding to messages. And the frightening thing about that was that Wickham had that person trying to infiltrate anti-government movements in the US.

"Now, what we would like to do is this," said Green. "Wickham is on ... leave. We want to assign his two staff to your joint group with Security Branch. *Assign* in the technical, personnel records sense of the word. You will order them both to return back here as quickly and ... quietly ... as possible. With the person in Washington, that should be simple enough. She'll fly into Toronto. She will either have her Republic passport with her, or we can provide a replacement to be waiting for her at the airport. Field Branch will provide a flight back here." Gorsky was taking notes on her phone.

"Now the other person. Captain Gorsky, we'll need your people to attempt to locate him. We'll wait until we know where he is, at least, before we decide any next steps. I'm sending the names and the personal details to Klein, now."

"All right, doctor," said Klein. "Two things. Can we assume Personnel is making the reporting changes?"

"Yes."

"And as of this morning, it's *Major* Gorsky. There'll be the usual announcements, including her group over here being moved up to Brigade level. That's all happened, literally, this morning."

"I was not aware of that."

"It's all been done in the last few days," said Gorsky. "Just official today. It doesn't have any effect on the relationship between your Department and ours."

"Well. Were we notified?"

"Yes," Klein said. "I was consulted."

"Hmm. Very well. My priority is closing out this situation that Wickham left us. Nothing else is really a concern, right now. Please keep me informed as you go forward." The call ended.

"Do you have to deal with him often?" asked Gorsky.

"No. And if he looks in his messages, he'll find that he *was* informed about your changes. By me. But he can't do anything about it, even if he wants to. It's an SB action, and my group's funding comes down a different path than his."

"Well, I'll get people working on the second person. Are you going to talk to the first one?"

"Yes. One thing I'd like to know is how she got down there in the first place. If she took a commercial flight to Canada, Finance would have seen it. And of course, a flight from there to Washington would show up, too. But going to Canada ... well, even Field Branch bills us for taking people back and forth to Maple Syrup Tastings."

"To what?"

"That's a term we use for less-than-critical diplomatic travel to Canada. It sounds better than 'junket'."

===

Allen Posten. He looked at the name again, then closed the application. The phone in his hand was intended for use at border crossings, airports, railway stations: anywhere quick verification of identity was part of the workflow. Here, at his kitchen counter, he'd just used it to ensure that his Peninsular Republic passport was still operating. He locked both the passport and the phone back into a small steel box. Elsewhere in his possession there was another, much less capable phone, plus a US passport and an Indiana driver's license. All three of those belonged to "Richard Baker."

It was getting closer to the point where he'd need the PR device and the documents. For at least two reasons that he knew of, he might have to pack up and head north. One reason was predictable, and it depended on things working out the way he intended. Another was the opposite of that. He wasn't a chess player, but he knew some of the game's more expressive terms. *Endgame*, he thought.

Inside the box, his PR phone woke up. It began flashing a "CALL" message, on and off. But since it was inside the box, and because its sound volume was set to zero and its vibration turned off, Posten was not aware that he'd finally heard back from his supervisor. A supervisor, at least, although it was someone he'd never heard of; someone named Klein.

===

"Buttoned up?" Field Branch aircraft commanders weren't easily identifiable unless you could see the wings on their jacket pockets. There were two of them at the controls, both Lieutenants, and both presenting as female. A Sergeant standing at the cabin door said that, yes, everything was. Buttoned up. The officer in the right-hand seat relayed that information to the Control room, and the Sergeant went back into the passenger area.

"Strap in, please," he said, adopting an authoritative voice. There were three civilian passengers; they fumbled with their documents, briefcases, cups of coffee, etc. Outside, the Brazilian-made transport plane's propellers began to turn.

"Here we go," said one of the civilians. "History in the making."

"Let's hope so, anyway," said another. Seven hundred and fifty kilometers north-east, a conference room in a Canadian government building was being prepared. The next morning it would witness, for the first time in twenty-eight years, direct talks between officials of the Peninsular Republic and of the United States of America.

===

At roughly the same time, at a slightly shorter distance south-east, Katherine Connor jumped as her PR phone went off. She'd kept it out of its usual hiding place, covered with a magazine in case ... of someone ... who? ... coming in. None of the people she'd met in Washington would be remotely likely to drop by. But, still.

She picked it up, noted that the calling number was in Canada, and answered.

"Is this Miss Connor?" She said yes.

"You spoke to someone from the department earlier today, is that correct?" She said yes.

"Effective immediately, you report to me. The project you're associated with has been terminated. Do you have sufficient funds to purchase a flight to Toronto?"

She'd thought about that, already. "Yes. My card will work for that."

"When you have your flight arrangements, call me at this number. Get the earliest date available. You'll be met outside Canadian Customs by people who will provide further transport. You understand what I mean by that?"

"Yes. I'll get back to ..." The caller cut her off.

"Exactly. As you did travelling to your current location. Do you have any other questions?"

"Yes ... um, no, actually. I don't think so."

"All right. Again, make your travel arrangements quickly, and contact me at this number as soon as you have them. Goodbye."

In her office, in the basement of what had been a university art museum, Jeri Klein hung up. *Location spoofing*, she thought. *Comes in handy. I'll have to ask Gorsky if we can make it say First Circle of Hell.*

===

Gorsky's day went on, more or less as it started. It was after lunch before she could call Morgan Matthews. A Corporal picked up the phone, then turned it over to the Major. "Gorsky," she said. "I haven't heard from you for ages. What's up?"

"This is going to be a little funky," E began. "Bear with me. We're going through some personnel churn, down here. Our Colonel's out on Medical, probably for good. And we had a Brigadier retire on short notice. And the group I'm running was just declared to be a Brigade, and they gave me a red badge to go with it. So, short version: would you want to come down here and talk about running Second?"

"Running second what? ... Wait, Second Brigade?"

"Right."

"Oh ... wow. You kind of ... read my mind."

"Really?"

"I'm not in the back or anything, here. But, yes, I would certainly be interested in talking. To you?"

"No, to the poor soul who's handling two Brigades, plus the Division. Her name's Lena Kléber, and she would really like to talk to you. I'll tell her you want to hear about it, and she'll call you."

"That's great. And you're running a Brigade, too?"

"So-called. Right now, it's eighteen people. But who knows what the future may bring. I didn't know about any of this until Friday. We're trying to move really fast, and I'd love to have you down here. You and Kléber and me: what a team. We'd be the three gray sisters."

"What?"

"Greek mythology. Never mind. So, if you don't hear from Kléber, say, tomorrow, call me and I'll nudge her."

"All right. Thanks. Thanks a lot."

===

Phil Hallstatt was still on the road, interviewing people with the rank of Major, out in the numbered Divisions. They had to be people with time in grade and no black marks on their records. *At least two years. And no important screw-ups. And not touchy. That's all I ask.* Despite a national commitment to eliminate harassment, sexual or otherwise, in the workplace, things would still happen. And this new Colonel, whoever he or she turned out to be, was *not* going to do that kind of crap. *Not on my watch!*

He was aware that his boss, General Newhouse, still had some goals for him to accomplish, and he took that seriously. In meetings with her and with General Kydo and O'Neill, he'd heard them speaking right to the point, saying what needed to be said, laying out what had been done and what needed doing. All in their "I wouldn't be wasting our time with this if I wasn't sure," tone. When he tried to do that himself, somehow it didn't sound the same. And what he just couldn't do was the sarcastic or self-deprecating signoff. O'Neill, for example, would lay out half a dozen points, stress the important ones, and then say, "Or at least that's how it looks to my weary old eyes." Or something like that. Newhouse would come right back at him with a line of her own, and everybody would smile. He had serious trouble talking that way.

His partner, an art professor named Jerry Villars, was helping him with it, talking about how he'd learned to "vet" a sentence or an expression quickly, before saying it. The trouble, he'd said, was doing it fast enough that you can tweak it before it comes out. "Death to obfuscation," he'd say. "Kill the commas!" "Long live the simple declarative sentence!"

I'll try, thought the General. *I'll try.*

===

It was closing in on 1700 hours. Gorsky was trying to reduce the new situation to order, for some definition of "order." As she'd been advised, the main growth in her duties would be personnel activity. In theory, she wrote reviews of the people who reported directly to her and approved their reviews of those they managed. The ones she wrote would go up to the Division commander ... when there was one. At this point, she'd have just her Lieutenant to write up, and he wasn't due for months, anyway. By then, there was every reason to hope that there'd be a new Colonel, and she wouldn't have to try for a few minutes of Hallstatt's time.

But that was just performance. Even in a group with a handful of people, there were likely to be promotions due. And as had already been hinted, there might be an expansion of the group. That would mean mundane things like floor space, gear, maybe a second secure conference area ... oh, and security appraisals. How secure were things, anyway? Brigades routinely audited each other, across Divisions. So somebody from, say, Fourth Division would come and look over her shoulder, and eventually she'd return the favor. A line from a 1980s film crossed her mind: Sean Connery saying, "I could USE a little help!"

As she came to that point, the Senior ER person in the group tapped on the open door and asked if she had a minute.

"Sure, come on in." Sharon Christopher was an Analyst Three in External Relations' terminology: a senior, highly-cleared person, capable of both hands-on work and managing small teams. That was exactly her role in Gorsky's group; all the ER people were under her.

"So, about Meg Cordell," she said. "I told you, I hope, that she's about done with her National Service time. And she wants to transition?"

"You did. Fine with me."

"The trouble is, we don't have a slot for an Analyst 1. Doctor Klein hired a person into our last open position a couple of months ago."

"Oh, dear. I'd hate to lose ... wait." She began flipping back through pages on her screen. "Damn this ... Oh, okay, here we are. Approved headcount ... right! We've got a PFC job unfilled. Two of 'em, actually. Just now. Because, *poof*, we're a Brigade. And we're not going to find anybody at that level who knows what we do. We might get a Corporal or a Sergeant from another Division, but ... "

"So you could take her?"

"If she wants to, sure. Some more money, maybe not as much as with your side of things, but, hey, nice free uniforms. Saves on clothing."

"That's ... I'll ask her. And if she does... we come and talk to you?"

"Yeah. I'd have to go up the chain to add *new* slots ... I just learned that about five minutes ago ... but existing ones, it's up to me. And I don't think General Hallstatt is really going to have time to argue, not until he finds us a

Colonel, anyway. Oh, but get Doctor Klein's okay on it, though."

"Thanks. I'll see if Meg's still here. She usually stays a little late."

"Don't thank me. It's all in a ... first day's work."

===

In a stand of woods, well away from its owner's farm house and the road that ran by it, a group of twenty-three men were gathered closely together. Two of them seemed to be in charge, at least to the extent that they were doing most of the talking.

"Numbers," said one of the two. "We need to plan on seventy or so guys. This ain't a raid. We ain't goin' in, raisin' hell, and comin' back out. We're gonna need shifts, you know. Who's on duty, who ain't. Sleepin' or guardin'."

"And trucks," said his colleague. "Figure two guys each, gear and stuff in the back seat, in the truck bed, and all. That's thirty, thirty-five vee-hicles. All four-wheelers, too. And a few with blades ... triangular snow blades. Push through the brush, once we get over the highway."

"And some chainsaws, too."

One of the audience said, "Doug? What about that fence? On the border?"

"It's crap. Just chain link. Blades on the trucks. We'll bust right through it."

The other man, Lou, said, "Supplies. BYO rifles. And ammo. 5.56, unless you've got an AK. If that's what you got, all right. But we'd rather be standard. You know, standardized. Pistols? Nah. There's nothing concealed-carry about this. Don't bother with 'em."

"And food," Doug added. "Jugs of water. Canned rations if you got 'em. Or try to get some ASAP. Otherwise, anything dried or preserved. Figure on a week, at least. Before we can get any kind of regular delivery set up."

"How's that gonna work? If we can't go back across. Back here?"

"Couple of ways. One, that's part of the payoff for not closin' the freeway. We get supplies for not messin' with it. And two, maybe farther out, we get a deal with the Ree-public, up there. We hassle the US, and they don't have to. And maybe they can use some folks like us with their own little problems, too. Or maybe we just get stuff from them for not giving them trouble."

Doug spoke up. "Now, medical stuff. I'm sorry to have to say it, but if you've got real problems, or you're takin' lots of meds ... just don't come along. It's gonna be a while before we can set up things like that. For casualties, now, we need a first aid ... thing ... in every truck. Make sure you got one, and read the labels. The instructions, you know?"

"Okay. Anybody got anything else? Rich, you wanna say anything?"

"Nope. You covered it. Oh, communications. Make sure you got your phones and you got the comm group saved. Like we talked about. That's where a lot of the talking will be, once things kick off."

"All right. Let's get at it, gatherin' things up. We'll be pickin' a date real soon."

===

As Klein was leaving for the day, she got a call. It lasted just long enough for her to note a flight number from Washington Dulles into Toronto. It would arrive before noon. "Very well," she said. "You'll be met at the airport, as I described." The call ended. *That'll work. We'll have a plane up there and waiting for her.* She made a call to the Field Branch aviation command, then set out for home. *Now, let's see if Gorsky can find the other guy.*

===

Meg was not in the office. Instead, she was dropping in on one of the government health clinics. They were the public-facing, on-demand, routine-issues incarnation of the Department of Health. You visited them for minor complaints, referrals to more advanced care, and other routine topics. Meg hadn't been in one for some time, and she glanced at the signs above a series of check-in desks. *Ah,* she said to herself, and approached one.

"Good afternoon," the woman at the counter said. "Could you scan your ID for me?" Meg did. "Thank you." She looked at her display screen, leaning in slightly. It had been a long day, reading people's histories and symptoms. "Ms. Cordell... you don't have a lot of recent information here. Are you still living at ... " She read off an address.

"No, update that from my ID, please. I've moved to a new apartment."

"Fine... All right. Done. Now, what can I help you with?"

"I'd like to start taking Konstantin, again. I haven't been for ... let's see, five years, actually."

"Very well. Were you advised to stop taking it?"

"No. There just wasn't any ... need to."

"I see. We can do that." She swung her chair around, unlocked a cabinet with her ID, and picked out a small package. "Here we are. This is a ninety-day supply. Make sure you keep track. You can get more from any of our clinics."

"Thanks very much," Meg said. She put the box of adult female contraceptives in her shoulder bag.

"Have a nice evening," said the woman, smiling.

===

Tuesday

Most secure conference rooms look generally similar. An absence of windows, for one thing, was pretty much universal. Inside the walls, various kinds of shielding might be in place, minimizing audible and radio-frequency leaks. There would be varying kinds of locks on the doors, of course, and any networking was likely to be wired, not broadcast. Decor would vary with the national host and its culture, but for the most part, things were predictable. This one was no exception.

Although the room was being borrowed from the Canadian National Defense Headquarters, no one present was in uniform. All three of the nations represented were natively fluent in English; no translators were necessary. Canada, the host, had sent just one person, the United States had sent two, and the Peninsular Republic had a team of three.

"Having dealt with introductions, Canada proposes reviewing the agenda previously agreed." Nods around the table. "We agreed that each of the parties present will describe their nation's interests and reservations concerning closer cooperation among the parties. And we agreed that each party will present those outcomes to their respective governments, prior to a second set of talks."

One of the US representatives raised a hand. "My government asks that a second set of discussions be maintained as a desirable outcome, even if the above discussions do not demonstrate significant commonality of interest."

"Canada is willing to accept that."

"The Republic has no objection."

"Very well. Is there agreement on proceeding to an enumeration of interests and reservations, then?" There did seem to be agreement on that. "I will then ask the Peninsular Republic to address their reservations and interests."

===

Sharon Christopher had an early meeting, but it wrapped up quickly. *Let's get the Meg thing settled*, she thought. As usual, Meg was in her cube. She was looking at a stream of characters, just returned by a search script. "Having fun?" Christopher said.

"Oh, hi. These people ... " She gestured at her screen. "They think that's encrypted."

"And you know otherwise?"

"Oh, yes. I'm all over them. It'll take about five minutes, though."

"Good, I need just about that much of your time. Good news."

Meg typed something equally as obscure as its target, then stood up. "Ready."

In Sharon's office, she closed the door. "Not really secret, but you know, personnel talk."

"Oh, about staying on?"

"Right. I talked to Doctor Klein about you wanting to stay with us, and the problem is, we don't have a slot—you know, a position—approved at that level." Meg frowned. "But ... there's another way. The Captain ... I mean Major ... says you could go into Security Branch in the group ... the same group, just on her side of the aisle. Would you want to do that?"

"I'd be in Security? But still here?"

"Right. Almost the same thing, except ... free clothes."

"Oh. Uniforms."

"Right. You'd get a bit of onboard training. Like everybody, but since this isn't a cops and robbers part of SB, it'd be just a quick thing, who to salute, who you call Sir ... like that."

"Wow. That's ... " Her voice steadied. "Sure, I'd be happy to go that route."

She does that, Sharon thought. *Maybe a bit uncertain about something, then ... bang, decision.*

===

Katherine Connor's flight from Washington was a bit late. She came up from the plane on the walkway, and before she reached the end of it, a man in a very standard-looking dark suit/white shirt costume, asked her if she was Ms. Connor. She said, yes, she was. "Very good," he said. "If you'll come with me, you can skip the entry formalities."

That turned out to mean "not go through Canadian Customs." Instead, they stepped aside from the other passengers and he opened a door with some kind of electronic device. "This way, please." Three meters down a short hall, there was an elevator. He waved his own badge at it, and it opened.

"I do have some checked baggage," she said.

"I know. It'll be collected for you." The elevator started moving upward. "This takes us to a dedicated departure area; your belongings will be picked up and brought there."

"And then what?"

"As soon as you have your luggage, you'll board a PR aircraft. You're expected at the Capital District Air Base. People from Security Branch will meet you and provide transportation."
"To where?"

"I don't know that."

===

In the Canadian conference room, the afternoon was winding down. Among the initial agreements was a specification that this first meeting would be limited to a single day's talks, and it had gotten to the point where summaries were called for. Stripping away jargon and language, the sense was that the US was interested in a warming of relations with the Republic, perhaps extending to intelligence sharing in specific areas and topics. The Republic was primarily interested in a formal guarantee of its current borders with the US. There had never been a diplomatic conclusion, with the US specifically committing to, for example, the old Ohio and Indiana borders as a legal line in the sand.

Beyond that, there were vague hints that the PR, US, and Canada all had concerns regarding splinter political movements, the only difference being that the PR denied having any such groups, itself; its concerns were solely with those in the two other countries. And there was agreement to set another meeting, with a broader agenda and participation by higher ranking officials.

"Well, that was nice," said the PR's lead, as they were being driven back to the airport. "No one threw anything. No insults."

"It's remarkable how much difference a change in government can make," said the team leader. "Especially when it involves replacing idiots with reasonable, well-meaning women."

===

Message: "Gorsky! Thanks for the tip on Maj. Matthews. Talked. She's getting to Mac City now, flight down here early tomorrow AM. Looks good to me—have to make this place look good to her. Schedule coming to you yet this PM."

My, my. Kléber wasn't kidding when she said she could move people around. Maybe I'll volunteer to do the wining and dining. Gorsky was pleased, not only that there might be a candidate, but also that Matthews was willing to come clear down to the Capital for interviews. *She and Kristin were always friendly, and K really loves a chance to dine out on the government's nickel.*

===

Another trip on one of the little Brazilian planes; it was becoming a routine, although not quite a scheduled one. There were just two passengers, this time; a young woman and an official the crew saw almost every trip, taking documents and people back to the Capital. The woman had a couple of bags, stowed in the cabin, since there was no shortage of overhead space. The Legation staffer had his diplomatic document case. They were already at cruising altitude, pointing the nose south-west toward the Republic and its capital. The attendant, with nothing else to do, sat down, herself, saying, "Just about an hour. As usual. Call it 1700 hours."

Seventeen hundred ... five o'clock. I have to get used to twenty-four-hour time, again, Connor thought.

===

On another recruiting front, Hallstatt was preparing to head south. His swing through 5th and 6th Divisions, up at the tip of the Lower Peninsula, hadn't been a complete waste; there was a Major running one of 5th's Brigades who might, in a year or so, be ready for promotion. But not yet. Too tactical, still. *We're not giving these people enough big picture stuff. We used to do that ... I think.*

His next move involved a hop from Mackinaw City's air field, sitting right up at the Straits, down to Third Division's airfield at Bay City. *Fifty minutes, give or take,* he thought. Even when they were carrying brass around, the Republic's aircraft would almost always have some kind of "While you're at it..." tasks: people or gear, mostly, sometimes a bit of quick ground imaging. *I can read resumes,* he thought. *I hate reading resumes. Or ...* He stood up and retrieved his briefcase from the overhead. Even though there was no one else within four seats, he didn't leave things on the seat if they weren't in use. Habits were habits, after all.

Inside the case he had a classified document reader. He turned it on and watched it boot. It came up quickly and showed him a menu of the docs he'd selected. Halfway down the unsorted list, past several personnel files and some financial reports, there was a file named "NATO2 Position and Questions." *It'll keep me awake, anyway.*

===

There wasn't a separate medical organization, serving the Army of the Republic. The Department of Health provided some specialists in combat trauma, and they wore uniforms when they were acting with the AoR, but otherwise, the soldiers, sailors, and police received healthcare in the same way as anyone else. This afternoon, a cardiologist was seeing an older gentleman. He'd presented in the neurology group five months ago after experiencing symptoms that seemed neurological. He'd had some cardiograms and been referred to cardiology.

This new doctor looked at his chart: physically male; presents as male; age sixty-four years; no established partnership; no offspring ... the summary of a person's life, measured out in the coffee spoons of personal health information.

"Well, Colonel Lamoreaux, nice to meet you. How are you feeling?"

The patient said that he felt much as he always did. "Sometimes a little short of energy, I guess."

"Headaches?"

"Only from my staff."

The visit went on along those lines. Tests and imaging from the prior episode were inconclusive. The doctor listened to his heartbeat, looked again at the tests, and decided that another set of electrocardiograms in, say, three months, might be a good idea. The patient didn't have an opinion on that. "So I'll set those up, and we'll see you again in July. Take care." Colonel John Lamoreaux, Commander of Field Branch Division 2, picked up his hat and went back to the base.

===

"Good afternoon, Council Member. How are things in the citadel of our freedoms?" O'Neill was one of a very few people who spoke familiarly with Alistair Felix, CM. Almost anyone could have, but it was generally not done. Council was not an aristocracy; in a socialist country, that would have been theoretically deprecated. But its older and wiser members were given respect commensurate with their ability. And Felix was extremely able and somewhat older.

With O'Neill and a few others, he adopted a kind of rustic, backcountry affect, mostly for mutual amusement. "Well, good afternoon to you, sir. I hope I find you well. Things here are, I'm delighted to say, less obscure than usual. In fact, I have only one minor obscurity to discuss."

"I remain delighted to help. I wonder if it might be related to our massive neighbor to the south?"

"It is. And surprisingly, it doesn't seem connected with the little talks that we and they and our Canadian friends just had. Or perhaps it's intended to be a parallel topic. Let me summarize a kind of back-channel message I received this afternoon. Strangely enough, it was a phone call."

"Directly to you?" There wasn't really any reason why someone in the US couldn't call a PR Council Member, but it was one of those things that just didn't seem to happen.

"Yes. I was mildly surprised, I admit. It appeared, initially, to be a promotional call, offering me vacation property."

"I see." O'Neill didn't, in fact, see.

"But do you remember, back in the few months just after Separation, when we had a few informal contacts, still, down there? People who were sympathetic to our ... rebirth?"

"Ah, yes!" To his mild chagrin, O'Neill had not, in fact, remembered those brief, helpful communications, masked as marketing.

"This turned out to be from one of those people. A gentleman who was highly placed in their Commerce Department, then. He's now retired, he tells me, but he says the new Administration asked him to, as he put it, *touch base* with us. It had to do with some help we might provide. Help with some of their rowdy and enthusiastic opposition."

After another few minutes, Felix had to sign off. A committee meeting was about to start. He asked Otto to think about the topic, sharing it with General Newhouse if he thought it was worth her time. And not, he suggested, with External Relations. "I think," he'd said, "It's really a police and army problem, not diplomatic." O'Neill agreed.

===

At the Capital Airbase, Connor was met, right at the bottom of the steps down from the aircraft, by an older woman. "I'm Jeri Klein," she said. "We spoke on the phone. I have a car outside, and I've got a room for you at our offices."

"I'd like ... to understand ..."

"We won't be talking about anything concerning the work you were doing until we're in a closed area. Not even in the car. The driver isn't cleared for any aspect of this. In fact, assume no one is until I confirm that they are."

===

Evening. General Hallstatt set his travel bag and his briefcase down. All the SB Divisional headquarters had rooms for visiting officers, and none of them were luxurious. But after a really undistinguished meal at the Third Division mess hall and a half hour attending to issues other than recruiting a new Colonel, he didn't care about accommodations. For the first time since they began, he could see a possible conclusion to his recruiting efforts. Most of the afternoon had been spent talking with Major Steven MacDonald, and, *damned if it might not work,* he thought. The man had the time in grade—service as a Major for three and a half years, more or less—and in a Division that wouldn't collapse if it lost him. He was bright, calm, and ready for a move. And he wouldn't be hard to replace. *I can think of three people, at least, who could come over and do his job.* Third was not the biggest problem command in the country. Its old, crumbling cities were sorely depopulated, Council was working hard on ways to build up a tech-based economy for what remained, and what crime there was called for basic, benign police work. *Not hard to backfill that kind of slot if we hire this guy away.*

===

"Rich?"

"Yeah. Who else would it be?"

"Sure. Um, we got a couple of problems with the ... the gear."

"Okay, which gear?"

"The tractors. There's kind of a shortage."

"How much of a shortage?"

"Looks like we've got twenty-three so far, is all."

"But all the right size?"

"Yeah. Lou said he might be able to ... to borrow a few more."

"Borrow?"

"Sort of ... extended loan, kind of."

"I don't think that'll work. Let's ... give me a minute, here ..."

"Sure."

Allen Posten set his phone down. The gist of the conversation, phrased in the crude, word-substitution code he'd been able to impose on his contacts, was that they weren't able to round up the thirty-five to forty big pickup trucks the plan called for. And they might be able to get a few more illegally, i.e. by stealing them. *Not a good idea. Too many risks.* He didn't need this pause to use a calculator or to do anything, in fact. He just needed to make the caller wait long enough to believe he was carefully re-planning something. He picked the phone back up. "Let's go with what we've got. We can make some of 'em do double duty. We don't want to do any of that loan stuff."

"Okay. You sure?"

"I'm sure. How about the hand tools?"

"The what ... oh, the hand tools. No problem there. Got plenty."

"All right, good. Anything else?"

"Nope. I'll check with you and the other folks ... mid-day tomorrow."

"Bye."

Shortage of trucks, plenty of firearms and ammunition. Not a surprise. Allen's unconcern about logistics was rooted in a simple fact: he didn't *want* the operation to succeed. The bigger and more embarrassing a failure it was, the better. He just needed to make it happen and get the hell out.

===

It was past 2000 hours at The Sunset House. The last diners were gone, and the "Closed" sign was hung on the door. George and Ciela were at the bar, side by side, talking.

"Pure luck," George said. "The lake could have come up a bit more and taken over, all the way past the highway."

"It still could."

"Yeah. But not without notice. We'd know, a year or so in advance. At least."

"Probably true. We'd have enough time to figure out ... something. Both of us. What would *you* do?" she asked.

"By the time anything like that happens, I'll be old enough for retirement to kick in. Sell the movable assets, take the insurance on the building. Go somewhere a bit further from the Lakes. Maybe finally write that book I mentioned."

"I'd have to try ... another store, I guess. I'm not that old, yet. I'm just not sure what my next move would be."

"You could come with me." He held out his hand, and she took it in hers.

===

Wednesday

"Major Matthews? I'm Corporal Brannan. Major Kléber asked me to meet you. I have transport outside."

"Thanks. This is all the baggage I brought." *Some emotional baggage, I suppose, but ...*

Matthews was tall. That might be your first impression. Then you'd notice her dark, very straight hair, cut short and slicked down, almost to the point of ambiguity. Her eyes were blue, technically, but dark enough to look black under anything but strong light. And she kept her brows to a thin pair of arches, dark against a pale Caucasian forehead. Like so many people with multiple generations of North American ethnic blending, you'd have been challenged to define a background. *Western European* might be as close as you'd come. And if you'd asked, she'd have said, quite truthfully, "I really don't know much about my family."

In the car, the Corporal gave her a printed agenda. "The Major put this together for you. You'll see that you start with her, then you'll have time with the Lieutenants, then lunch ..." He went on. It was going to be quite a day.

===

Klein was in her office twenty minutes early. So was Gorsky, evidently, given that she answered her phone at once. "So, the DC person is back here?" Gorsky asked.

"She is. I picked her up yesterday evening. I assume you want to be on the phone? As opposed to coming over here?"

"That would be better. We've got a Second Brigade command candidate here. Kléber's seeing her first, but she'll bring me in at some point."

"Fine. What I want out of this young lady ... Katherine Connor ... is what Wickham told her she was supposed to be doing, and what information she actually got. And ..."

"And?"

"She was down there, trying to meet government people, before, during, and after the election. If she got anything after that ... well, management over here is quite interested in knowing about it. A lot more than about the old guys."

"Sure. Me, too, in fact."

"So, when she comes downstairs, I'll call you."

"Great." *Downstairs* was a reference to the topography of the ER headquarters building. Klein and her people were in the basement of what had been a university museum. The irony of the collections being moved to a nice new place downtown, and the old building filled up with diplomats and other questionable types was not lost on Gorsky, Klein, or anyone else.

===

Connor was given about fifteen minutes to grab and finish breakfast in the ER building's small dining area. Then the junior staff person serving as her chaperone brought her down to see Klein. Gorsky was already on the phone.

"The intention, here, is to straighten out what was going on with you, down in the US. I'm your new boss—you know that from yesterday. And on the phone's a colleague of mine. She needs to hear what we talk about, too. " She paused.

Gorsky said, "Hello."

"A few days ago, management here found out, for the first time, that Doctor Wickham had people outside the country. According to paperwork, you were supposed to be here, in this building, working with him on some research of his. Doing academic reviews of information, and summarizing them for him. Do you see why this caused some concern?"

"Well, yes ... if that was the ... expectation. That was never anything I discussed with him. Or anyone."
"Nothing about this being an assignment here? A research job?"

"No. Not at all."

"Do you have anything at all like a job description? Anything he gave you?"

"No, he ... He said there wasn't one."

"How were you contacted? How did you know the job even existed?"

"He said he'd seen me on the site ... the list of people who'd applied for jobs."

"Oh." Klein paused and rubbed her temple with two fingers. "I haven't seen that site in a long time. Let's have a look at it." She put her display up on the screen behind her. "Your job won't be there, of course, but I'd like to see what the applications look like." The main page was completely ordinary, a government department's recruiting site. Klein selected Entry Level Positions. "*Oh. Did yours look anything like this?*"

"I guess ... yes, it did. I remember putting it together."

The primary feature of the page, providing the credentials of a young woman who was graduating from a four-year International Studies program, was a color photograph, fifteen centimeters square, full face, and professionally shot. She was smiling broadly.

"Did you have a photo like that? On yours."

"Yes. We were advised to make it attractive ... Oh. Oh, I see. I think I see what you mean. I ..."

"Don't feel bad. Not everybody flips through, looking for the big smile and the bright eyes. But ... what?" Connor was actually crying.

"Do you know what I was ... doing? Down there?"

"Well, not completely."

"He ... just about ... almost literally ... told me to get information by sleeping with people."

===

Matthews came out of the First Brigade restroom. Her first two hours with Kléber had been absorbing; the two of them had absorbed as much as they could, one from the other. On her part, Matthews perceived Kléber to be highly engaged with SB, the Division, and its people. The heart of it appeared to be a kind of guardianship; holding chaos at bay, keeping wolves from doors, being the dogs that circled around the flock. What she couldn't decide was whether this was a permanent state of mind or an artifact of doing three jobs at once. For her part, she wasn't certain what impression she'd made.

I think ... actually I guess, I may have gotten a point or two across. Kléber seemed to focus, properly enough, on Second Brigade. It needed, she said, someone willing to analyze, not just react. She'd said that at least two different ways, and Matthews had translated it, the second time, as a criticism of the previous Major.

"Are you saying," she'd said, "that it needs someone who can change things when they need changing?"

That had apparently been precisely what was meant. Matthews proceeded to describe some events in which she'd made changes, some of them on the fly. And she got in a mention of Gorsky.

"I got her promoted early, because we had a case that needed a little more clout. That was before Big Bay and all that crap with Naval Branch." Kléber nodded and agreed that boosting subordinates when it was right was exactly the kind of thing she meant.

Well, she flexed her shoulders and stretched her arms over her head, *now, we go meet the team.* Outside, two dogs were chasing each other around the square, barking. You could hear it faintly, even inside.

===

Connor was given a visitor office, a desk and a machine, and she was directed to start writing a description of her work with the department to date. Klein called Gorsky again. "So ..."

"So."

"What I really care about now," Klein said, "Isn't so much Wickham but the other guy down there in the US. Doing who knows what. And not answering his phone."

"Yeah. And who is he sleeping with?"

"Is there anything your guys can do, just with the phone number? Like, see if it's still alive? Or left up here, somewhere?"

"We can try. But I got all excited about a phone contact once, and it turned out to be in a city dump truck, headed for the landfill. It helped, though. Once a couple of troopers dug it out."

"I'd settle for that. But Connor kept hers with her. So my guess would be, he still has it and won't answer if it isn't Wickham. Or he's keeping it turned off, or it's out of battery or something."

"Or in a garbage truck."

"Yeah, okay."

"But ... what's Wickham's status, right now? Can we get him to call? From his phone?"

"If he's willing."

"Can we, perhaps, influence him to be willing?"

"You'd think you were a cop or something. That's what I was hoping you'd say."

"You get him over there in a room. He shows up, sits down. Then I drop in, and maybe I bring one of Kléber's more squared-away Sergeants with me. Just to stand there and look menacing."

"Good. I need to talk with my boss, but then let's do it."

===

O'Neill was, for a change, physically present in the Army of the Republic's command facility. "General," he said, "It's nice to see you in person for a change."

General Newhouse smiled. "Likewise, Otto. Likewise."

"I mentioned to you on Monday that I'd received a call about a potential problem with External Relations and one of their people. This was a thing that could cause discontent between us and our neighbors, just when things seem to be thawing a bit."

"Right."

"Well, I haven't heard anything more about that. But yesterday, Councilman Felix mentioned a call from one of our old original supporters in the US. The gist of it was that the US believes we might be able to lend a hand with their right-leaning population."

"Yow."

"As you say, *yow*. On the one hand, we have efforts to improve our somewhat tense relationship with them. On the other, someone in ER was doing things that could tend to do the opposite. And on the third hand, they've expressed an interest in jumping the gun, I suppose you could say, on the improving part."

"What did Felix think about it?"

"He doesn't tend to ask advice, at least from you and me, unless he genuinely wants it. So I conclude that he hasn't fully decided."

"All right, putting my analytic hat on: it could be real, someone trying to get early help ... or help before the diplomatic stuff goes public. Or ... it could be bogus. In several ways."

"Or," said O'Neill, "It could be someone caught off balance by the election, trying to demonstrate initiative."

"Or ... how about this? A very subtle warning-off? Don't be doing any more of this stuff. The Wickham stuff."

"Or a less subtle trap? Let's see if we can get the Republic to stick its neck out before there's any agreement?"

Newhouse put her hands together, fingers laced, and rubbed them back and forth across her head, closing her eyes as she did so. "Let's set up a call with Felix. I think he should make the contact. Find out what their going-in proposition is, anyway. You or I might scare them off."

===

"Green? Can I have a word?" Peter Lorman was Klein's *de jure* boss—the person her record said she reported to. Doctor Green wasn't especially happy to see him, but there was no obvious way of avoiding it. "Of course."

"I wanted to bring you up to date on James Wickham and this unusual group of his. He's going to be given a chance to explain what it was all about, and it may amount to nothing, but because there could be problems, I'm going to keep all the discussions strictly in my area. Security Branch will be present, too. But there's no need for you to spend more of your valuable time on it."

"I'm not sure I agree with that. It involves my budget, after all."

"Yes, exactly. That's what the Department Chair pointed out. She's anxious that we resolve this without any suggestion of improper use of funds, lack of supervision, all those unpleasant things. Especially as we're all trying to concentrate on the new initiatives."

"I'd like to speak to her. I'm not convinced that this is the proper way to proceed."

"Of course. Feel free to contact her. Although you will recall that she's never particularly fond of changing a decision, once it's made. Anyway, just thought I'd drop by and bring you up to date. Have a good day."

===

Gorsky had spent forty-five minutes with Matthews, Kléber being called away to deal with a Divisional budget question. Nothing that was said really changed either person's mind about the job. Matthews wanted to have it, and Gorsky wanted the same thing. "Are you coming back in tomorrow?"

"So far, yes. I think Major Kléber wants to talk to you and the Captains together, so there probably won't be a decision, yet today."

"Well, I'm on your side. You're what we need. And think of the fun we'll all have, breaking in a new Colonel. If we ever get one."

"That would be fun, wouldn't it? And what's that bit? In Macbeth? About three witches? Double, bubble...?"

"Right. We could get pointy hats and have cookouts.

You know, with big kettles of something. Anyway ... Kristin and I want to take you to dinner. I should know this, but is there anything you don't eat?"

"Not on an ethical basis. I don't really crave big steaks, but I'm omnivorous, otherwise."

"Fine. I tasked her with picking a place. She's more of a socialite than I am. And I still have to go over to another department, yet today. I'll be back, and by then Kristin will know where we're going."

===

"Quick favor?" Gorsky stuck her head around Kléber's door.

"It'll cost you."

"Bill my account. I need to borrow a non-com for about an hour. Somebody really squared away. No-nonsense. And can keep his or her mouth shut."

"Hassan Brooke. Best match for that I've got. Right down the hall, and tell him I said he's all yours."

"Thanks. I'll loan you a really geeky looking software engineer, any time you need one."

Theatre, Gorsky thought. *Way, way off-Broadway.* She located Brooke, and he was everything the Major had promised. She explained that he needed to accompany her to ER headquarters, stand by in a meeting, and unless specifically directed, do nothing else. "Of course, Major," he said, reaching for his hat.

They walked the few blocks to External Relations. People in uniform were commonplace, wandering around the Capital, and no one paid any attention to another two of them. They went in at the side entrance she normally used to connect with Klein; her badge allowed her to authorize another party. The meeting with Wickham was a few doors down from Klein's office, and she was coming out as they appeared.

"Very nice," she said, looking at Brooke. "Have you explained what we're doing?"

"No, go ahead."

"Well, Sergeant, Gorsky and I and one of our senior people will be discussing things with someone. We anticipate that he'll cooperate with us, and we felt that having someone else from SB in the room might help ensure that he will."

"Yes, sir. Major Gorsky indicated that."

"All right, then. Let's go."

===

Rich and Lou were sitting in Lou's truck, in a parking lot. Lou was the member of the group who, more than anyone else, was emerging as a leader or at least an influencer. They were parked — pulled over, really — along a county road, North 1050 East. "We ran out o' people to name roads after," Lou had explained. Ahead of them, the pavement went under the Indiana Toll Road.

"Yeah," said Rich. "So what we want to do, I say, is bring most of the guys over here and come up this way. Under the highway. And on up North."

"Not through the fields, back there?" Lou nodded west, toward the crossing they'd been discussing.

"Nope. The river. The damn river is in the way. And I was looking at it online ... what we thought was a bridge, by that last house, isn't. It's just a walkway, like a dock, almost. No way to get trucks across that. But it doesn't matter. I looked at the east/west roads up there." He pointed ahead. "The first one we come to, if we're going north from here, Greenfield Road? ..."

"That's the border."

"The *north edge* of it is. The fence is outside the ditch and everything. On the north. The road's still open. We can just go under the highway here, straight north, nothing on either side, up to Greenfield, then we go west, all the way to where we were goin' to cross, quick right, plow through the fence, and that house is right there. No brush bustin' at all."

"That house" was a small farm where Greenfield Road became a driveway. It backed up against the Cub River Nature Area, just a few meters north of the border. It had been the group's target for some time, but getting there had been an optimistic narrative of smashing trucks through mature woods and over a small river. This route, on the other hand took them out of the US on an established if seldom used road, and it only called for bashing through one four-meter fence.

"Yeah, maybe that's smarter. We can take our time building a bridge or something. But what about this?" He pointed down, meaning the road they were on. "Do we need to block this off?"

"We could. But think about the roads down this way. There's nothing but farms. Closest town is Orland, over there." He nodded at the right side of the truck. "By the time they got even a sheriff's car over here and up to Greenfield, we're out of the US. Off limits."

"And the guys up there? In the Ree-public?"

"Long way for them. Clear over in Sturman, goin' west. And farther than that, off east. In Riverside."

"Like the TV show?"

"What?"

"There's a town called that?"

"Says so on the map, anyway."

===

It was one of the several more formal conference rooms, up on the first floor of the ER building. "Well, we're all here. Let's get started." Peter Lorman was in his neutral mode. Although he would never think of eating during any kind of formal event, butter wouldn't have melted in his mouth, had there been any to do so. "Introductions.

This is Doctor Wickham, Doctor Klein"—he nodded at Jeri—"Major Gorsky from Security Branch, and Sergeant Brooke. And of course, I'm Peter Lorman." Wickham looked nervous. Brooke was not actually required to stand, but he still looked quite severe, even seated.

"Now, what we need to resolve, if we can, is a set of misunderstandings related to work assignments for two of our employees. These people, Ms. Connor and Mr. Posten, were hired by Doctor Wickham. The posts into which they were hired were listed as Procedural Assistant One. The 'one' is a ranking, of course, indicating an entry-level position." No one had anything to say.

"Unfortunately, some sort of error took place, with the result that both of them were assigned to travel to another country and to attempt to make contacts among the citizens and residents there."

"When this came to light, it was obvious that the first thing we needed to do was contact them and give them instructions to return to the Republic as soon as possible. That was accomplished easily enough with one of them, Ms. Connor, but we have not been able to get in touch with Mr. Posten. Naturally, that raises concern about his safety."

"Excuse me," Wickham said, "I don't know why you wouldn't have been able to contact either of them. I provided their contact information to Doctor Klein as I was directed to."

"Doctor Klein, is that the case?"

"I have the number, and I've called it repeatedly. But it's never been answered. I wonder whether he doesn't want to respond to a number he doesn't know."

"Doctor Wickham, do you think that might be the case?"
"I ... I never advised him to do that. He might be concerned ... about security, I suppose."

"Can I suggest," said Gorsky, "that we simply try it? That we ask Doctor Wickham to call? And if he gets the subject to answer, get him headed home *at once*?"

"And make sure he knows about the change in ... reporting? That he works for me, now?"

"Doctor Wickham?" said Loman.

"I really don't want to be involved any longer in something that's outside my ... authority. I don't think it's in my best interest or that of the ..." He was probably about to say "the Republic," but Gorsky cut him off.

"Fine. Refusing to cooperate with an investigation is a level 2 offense. Sergeant ..." Brooke stood up.

===

"Thanks very much, Brooke. If the Army had a medal for acting, I'd put you in for it."

"It was a pleasure, sir. Happy to assist."

Jeri Klein and Gorsky had walked the Sergeant to the exit, the ER building being rather labyrinthine. "So," said Klein, "that was a partial success, anyway."

Doctor Wickham had thrown in his hand immediately. Using his official phone, he'd called Allen Posten—aka Rich Baker—and got no response. He left a message explaining that he, Wickham, was no longer in charge, and that the young man should suspend all activities and come home. In fact, the last part of that was, rather quaintly, "alas, suspend what you're doing." Wickham was then convinced to describe in full exactly what Posten and, by the way, Katherine Connor were supposed to be doing. As Klein said, the process worked well enough; the outcome was appalling.

Back in Klein's office, summarizing it with Lorman, she ticked off issues. "Everything has to be seen in the light of warming relations with the US. Just when it looks like they might want our help with things, one, we sent someone down there to provoke right-wing idiots into hijacking the Indiana Turnpike. Two, we've lost touch with him. Three, it appears to have been a research project, carried out without ER or anyone else knowing it was happening. Four, we don't know any more about it than that."

"And five," Gorsky added, "He recruited a PR citizen to poke around Washington, seeing who she could engage in pillow talk."

"I think that's an accurate summary," said Lorman.

"I'd just add—and this is no concern of the US—that it was done illegally. There was misuse of funds, for one thing. And I noted, just before the meeting, that our Charter—External Relations' *raison d'être*—forbids any contact, visual, virtual, auditory, physical, etc., with another nation without authority of the Director and The Council. It's a *verum non no*."

"A what?" Klein said.

"A real no-no."

"Can I assume that sometime in the near future, I should ask one of our boots-on-the-ground Brigades to arrest Wickham? Actually?" Gorsky looked eager; it had been a while since she'd done any real police work.

"I should know this," Lorman said, "but is there something just short of that? A *confined to quarters* approach? So that he can't just vanish?"

"Flight Risk Detention. He can stay home, but with observation. We can do that."

"Doctor Klein?"

"Fine with me."

"I'll make a phone call," Gorsky said. "Oh, and I have to keep reminding myself: I work for General Hallstatt, now, at least for a while. I should probably let him know." No one objected.

"And I'll speak with Doctor Green," said Lorman. His affect was formal and with an added touch of regret. Inwardly, he was looking forward to that conversation.

===

The Capital City's Downtown was clearly happy about the moderating weather. Sidewalk tables were showing up, although those with local weather experience tended to go inside. Rain was always a dice roll, in early spring. Kristin had picked one of her "out of town guest" restaurants, quiet but cheerful, with excellent but not flamboyant food.

Matthews had been particularly nice to her when she and Gorsky were beginning their partnership. She'd helped find them their rental house, and as a matter of absolute, unquestionable coincidence, an SB supply truck had just happened to have room for a box of Kristin's cooking gear when it had to be picked up from the Mackinaw Airbase. Besides that, she was delighted with the three witches concept.

The conversation had begun lightly, skipping around among Education Department gossip, Gorsky's new badge, hints of a thaw with the US; for once, neither of her companions knew much more than Kristin did about the latter, at least publicly. E, of course, knew things about it, but only as something that could be good and was not to be endangered until proven bad. The waitress knew Kristin, and she brought the wine list automatically. It wasn't until dessert that she realized Matthews hadn't had more than a sip or two.

Gorsky, on the other hand, was watching for indications of confidence about the job. It was hard to assess; Matthews seemed happy enough and hadn't brought it up, except for a mention of it having been a long day. E decided not to go into it, unless her colleague wanted to. And then, of course, she did.

"E," she said, "I mentioned when you called me that this was ... welcome. I meant it. I really want to get out of Seventh."

"Okay."

"Full disclosure, I stumbled into a bad thing, I guess. A thing is what it became." She paused. "Do you want to hear this? You don't have to. It's a personal ... failure."

"Anything you want to say, if *you* want to say it."

"I met a guy. Up there. And you know what that place is like. There's nothing to do. Unless you're heavily into wandering around in the woods, just nothing. And if there was, there was nobody to do it with. And I met this guy."

Kristin was using her listening-to-every-word affect. E just nodded.

"And he was ... I heard some of the women in the base talk about men who were *flannels* – guys who wore flannel shirts and boots and ... I don't know ... chopped down trees, I guess. He was one of them. And ... do you shock easily?" A negation.

"He was ... good in bed." Blank expressions. "But he was a jerk. And a drunk. The son of a bitch finally tried to hit me. I put him on the floor, got cuffs on him—yes, I was carrying handcuffs around the apartment—and I got my most discreet NCO to come and get him. But ..."

E closed her eyes tightly, then opened them again. "And then, things weren't good, I bet."

"Right. Things weren't good. I wasn't an officer and a gentleperson anymore."

"And you never got a Brigade. Bastards."

"Yeah. So ... don't do anything about this you wouldn't have, already, without hearing all that."

"I won't. It doesn't change my mind. We don't just need *somebody*, we need you."

===

Hallstatt's last official act of the day was to look at messages from his direct reports. *Gorsky? Why is she messaging me ... oh, right.* He'd managed to forget, for the moment, that she was reporting to him until there was a new Colonel. He opened the text. *Holy ... Rogue ER guys?* He responded "understood, carry on." He forwarded E's message to General Newhouse. And then to Otto O'Neill.

===

Thursday

Morgan Matthews dressed in her room; visiting officers' quarters at the SB Capital HQ were not luxurious by some standards, but not primitive either. For Matthews, it was beyond adequate. In Seventh Division, she had a bed and some clothes hooks in the same ex-public-school building where she worked. This was an economic consequence of her collapsed relationship. *Fingers crossed*, she thought. She had a 0745 meeting with Kléber. The outcome would determine the rest of her career. *It'll be here or anything else I can find down south. I hope it's here.*

Upstairs in the First Brigade command area, Kléber was already on deck. She'd exchanged messages with Hallstatt, read the reactions from the Second Brigade Captains, and had Gorsky's recommendation up on her screen. *Okay, ready for that meeting*, she thought. A quick glance over the night's report summaries—essentially, just headlines in the form location-time-crime—showed her nothing dramatic. *Drunks and traffic.* Looking at her messages, she saw that Personnel wanted periodic reviews of a Captain and two non-commissioned officers. The one for the Captain, she did owe them. She'd have to ping the appropriate Lieutenant about being late with his NCO appraisals. And at the top of it all, her calendar showed a remote chat with the first Colonel candidate that Hallstatt felt was worth the time. *Not too bad a day. Could actually be pretty good.*

===

Newhouse, Hallstatt, and O'Neill were all up, well before the Republic's normal 0830 starting time. "I pulled

General Kydo into this," Newhouse said, "And she'll be dialing in ... ah, now." In fact, all four of them were present remotely. "Based on two different threads in the last few days, we have ... something. Something to deal with."

"I agree," said O'Neill. "At least two vectors of something are diverging, converging, or emerging. And when I recognize situations like that, I usually feel that action of some kind is called for. The primary question, though, is *what?* What are the situations, and what is the action? General Hallstatt, could you give us a summary of the thing you learned yesterday?"

"This is a danger-of-pissing-off-the-US issue," Hallstatt said. "We didn't worry about that too much, before this, because we'd *really* pissed them off, already. Thirty-some years ago. But now, we need to try not to. The summary is, a guy in External Relations set up a rogue operator in a border state and lost contact with him for a while. And what he was supposed to be doing—the guy down there—was to encourage a right-wing group to invade us." No one on the call looked even slightly happy.

"Set aside for now the what-were-they-thinking analysis," Newhouse said. "We'll get to that in due time. The reason this whole thing would, as Phil put it, *piss off* the US, is that their new government is trying to warm things up with us ... at least they seem to want that." Newhouse was out of uniform, still wearing a bathrobe. "Otto?"

"And," said O'Neill, "As all that was going on, Council Member Felix has gotten some extremely backchannel contacts from people in the US Government, suggesting the possibility of our acting *with* them against their right-wing groups. Or some of them, anyway."

Kydo leaned in toward her screen. "There are entire states in the US that could be considered right-wing groups. Do we know any specifics?"

"Not yet, no." Hallstatt raised his hand, making a "small" symbol with thumb and forefinger. "According to the jackass in ER—his name is Wickham—it's a small bunch of people, out in farm counties. Right at the border, straight north of Fort Wayne. Just a bit east of Sturman, on our side."

"Second Division. Colonel Lamoreaux," General Kydo said. "I have a suggestion. We put him, personally, on alert for this. He's got the closest force ready to react."

"But ... satellite info. US satellites, I mean. Picking up on that?" General Newhouse wasn't at her aggressive peak at this hour of the morning.

"No troop movements yet. We just tell Lamoreaux to be ready. In fact, we have him prepare for a training event. One Brigade, getting ready to simulate a response to a border incident. And when we know more, we give him a target area." Kydo always gave the impression of preferring action to analysis, and it wasn't just an impression. "And if the US detects it, let them. We do this all the time, all over the country. Drills and practice."

"That might be a good thing," O'Neill said. "In a way, whatever they observe, we're not doing anything overt, and we're also signaling that we can, if we have to. Do something overt, that is."

Kydo raised her eyebrows. "Shall I?" Newhouse nodded. "One concern," Kydo added, "Lamoreaux is not a young man. But he seems to be capable. And the Division is in good condition."

O'Neill rubbed his eyes. "Very good," he said. "The message we really do *not* want to send, I think, is 'Some unknown number of far-right US citizens will attempt to occupy a position inside our borders so that they can stage attacks on a major east/west interstate highway. And we suggested it.' Agreed?"

===

In its lonely metal box, Allen's phone sat quietly. Allen himself had taken a shower, dressed, and was eating his usual inexpensive breakfast. Early the day before, he'd tried calling Wickham, hoping to get his cash problem dealt with. As usual, no answer. *I should check. He might have called while I was out.*

He opened the box. *Finally!* There had been a call. The number was right. Would Wickham be up and around, already? *Early, but ...* He touched the message button and listened. Thirty seconds later, he set the phone down. *Oh, hell!*

===

Meg's commute into the office was a matter of a block's walk, then a fifteen-minute tram ride. Sometimes there was someone she knew and a conversation; today was a day for a phone call. It would be to a woman named Karen Mather, the closest thing she had to a mother. Karen would be up; she had a house full of confused young people to manage. Meg knew what she wanted to say to Karen; she wasn't entirely sure what Karen herself would have to say.

===

When Matthews arrived at First Brigade Command she was welcomed by Kléber's desk Corporal. "Go right in, Major." She noted that Gorsky was there, too. *Good sign? Maybe.*

"We have quite a day," Kléber said, "and I want to thank you for, I hope, taking some of the stress off it. Gorsky, here, as usual, has some really interesting things going on, and I'm going to share in some of it, I was just told. Anyway, we'd like to see you move into the Second Brigade position as soon as possible." If you were watching closely, you might have noticed Matthews inhaling a bit more deeply than a second before. And her shoulders straightening. "And in fact," Kléber went on, "If you're willing, how does a start date of RIGHT NOW sound?"

"Thank you," Matthews said. "I imagine there's some paperwork regarding my transfer? But other than that, RIGHT NOW would be just fine."

"Oh, there's paperwork, all right," said Gorsky. "And since you're a Major already, and you've been trained to do that stuff, your first job is to fill it out."

===

Con call number two. I should keep count of 'em. Hallstatt watched as Kléber and Gorsky appeared on screen. "Good morning, two-thirds of my Capital command. Did Matthews accept?"

"Happy to say, yes she did," said Kléber. "And she looked happy about it, too."

"Good. Thanks, Gorsky, for the recommendation. Anyway, folks, here's the Colonel situation. I've got a candidate from up in Third. Steve MacDonald. He's in charge of their Second Brigade, now, and he's technically ready. Time in grade, experience, all that. But more to the point, he's wasted where he is. And he comes across as smart. So I want to dial him in, here, in just a minute. Anything you want to say, first?"

"Not from me." Kléber was primarily interested in getting someone at least trainable into the Colonel's chair.

"And I hope to be as little trouble as possible, for him," E said. That was a sincere hope.

"Okay. By the way, I had a chat already this morning about ... your message last night, Gorsky. I'll send you a summary, once I get through this and other conversations. Let's bring MacDonald into this."

===

Allen Posten was looking at his pair of wallets. One held a small amount of US identification: a driver's license and firearms carry license from the State of Indiana, one of the new US national healthcare cards, a picture of a miscellaneous woman, picked at random from the Internet; enough detail to pass for someone without gainful employment in the Midwestern United States. The other wallet held all the things he'd need to get into the Republic. If he could. He put that one back into the metal box with the phone, but instead of leaving the box in the apartment, he put it in a plastic grocery bag and took it with him, out to his truck. The truck already had a couple of changes of clothing, stuffed behind the rear seat.

It wasn't a long drive to the Hall's Lake Tap, but he planned on a slightly longer route, north and around, so that he could drive by it from behind, first, just to be sure there weren't any unusual vehicles. Vehicles other than large pickup trucks, for example.

He checked the fuel gauge. After the conversation at the Tap, he had another little drive in mind. Five miles or so by way of N 1050 E, up under the I-80 bridge, and along the PR border just a bit west — the same route as planned for the attack. It would be just a peek, enough to make see if a man on foot could get over or under the fence, quickly and without a lot of noise or light. That one word — "alas" — in Wickham's voicemail suggested this little reconnaissance. Its prearranged meaning was "Ignore everything else in this message, carry on." The only reason it would have been there was that something had gone wrong, but not so wrong as to cancel the plan. *I'm really on my own, here. I have to make my own plans. I have to invade the Republic, too, just to get home.*

===

"This is Karen... Hi, Meg." For Karen Mather, a call from one of her former ... rescues ... was always a mixed blessing. It might mean anything: good news, bad, strange, the whole spectrum of circumstances that the Republic's population of emotionally uncertain young people could experience. It took about two seconds to determine that Meg's call was none of those common categories. As Meg said more, this call resolved itself into another well-known pattern: *I'm going to do something. Any advice?*

She listened to a few sentences, well-formed and coherent. These conversations tended to be less structured than that; the descriptions of the thing the caller had already decided to do weren't always very well formed. Meg's were, psychologically and physically. She had contingency measures in place, the *what I'll do if* ... plans. And the preparations already made were both necessary and sufficient.

"To sum up," Karen said, "You ran into somebody on a tram. You're on your own, doin' your National Service. He's here, in town, doin' counseling. You're a grown up, so's he. You want to know what I think about you gettin' together. In a physical sense, at least. Right?"

"Karen. It's not that *cold*. Is it? Did I sound like that?"

"I've heard guys talk about girls less dispassionately."

"Well, I don't ... I'm starting not to think *dispassionately*. As much."

"About time. You're what, twenty-five? But you want some advice?"

"Yes. Please."

"Okay. Fun is one thing. Long term is another. And you're not the only one who can get hurt. If it doesn't work out. And it might not. No way to be sure. Just don't spend time on blame. Blame for him, blame for yourself. Just move on."

"But ... what if it *does* work out?"

"Well, then, you don't need advice, right? That's the definition of it workin' out."

"Okay. I see that. I think I can ... work with that."

"Good. One thing. Don't get pregnant."

"Karen! I wouldn't! I'm ... prepared."

"Okay, girl. When the dust settles, let me know how it went."

===

"Good morning, Major," said Hallstatt. "I'm online with Major Kléber and Major Gorsky. That's First and Third Brigades, respectively. And I'm happy to say we just brought on a Second Brigade commander, Major Morgan Matthews. She's working through the formalities of transfer, right now."

"Good morning, in return." On screen, at least, MacDonald looked quite soldierly. He was medium-brown-skinned, with black hair just starting to recede, and he wore an almost British-looking military mustache. As with Gorsky, there were eastern-western genetics in play. And at a guess, you'd put him in his mid-forties.

The General essentially gave the floor to his Majors. Kléber threw a couple of easy pitches, then brought out her key question, "The Capital's got a mix of people, more than the combinations I see when I look at Third Division's demographics. How would you modify your command technique to match up with a community full of academics, technicians, professionals, government folks, all living alongside people who ... aren't those things?"

"A good question. I gave that some thought when the General first contacted me, and the answer I came up with was simply that a change would be a mistake. For day-to-day policing, it *has* to be the same, whether the subject is a confused youth or a Department Head."

"Okay. From your experience in Third, do you have people who you consider good for one kind of investigation, and others with different ... abilities?"

"The Brigade's responsibility is divided among parts of cities—the urbanized places—and the physically larger, demographically smaller rural areas. I try to rotate individuals into and out of both kinds of ground. The goal is to have all parts of the Brigade, right down to the team level, ready to act fairly and effectively anywhere they might be needed. I won't claim that we've completely succeeded with that, but it's our goal."

"What kind of interaction with your Divisional head do you have?"

"Formal reporting, of course, but I've pushed for more two-way traffic, more *we should be doing...* than *here's what we did.* I believe we've established a good relationship and a sound mutual understanding."

"Gorsky?"

"Major, as I'm sure General Hallstatt told you, my group is an anomaly, and it's also an experiment. Plus, I share its command with External Relations. And there are ... evolutionary ... changes being discussed. How much of that would you want to be involved in?" *That's a leading question,* E thought. *How'll he handle it?*

"Frankly, I see the initial challenges for someone coming into command of Capital Division as understanding the mass mission, the day-to-day enforcement of the laws in the country's largest city. The General gave me an overview of your Brigade, and for one thing, its mission is far outside my experience. And for another, he says it's operating at a high level of efficiency. So I would see my role as providing administrative assistance, helping with personnel and budgetary topics—the things that might tend to distract you from your mission. And as your group evolves, that formula could evolve along with it.

But always with the goal of supporting the work you and your people do."

Oh, he's good. He talks the talk. "My goal," she said, "Of course, is to work closely at the outset with a new Divisional Commander, laying out the levels of clearance necessary, getting the briefings done, and trying hard to work all that in around your takeover of, as you say, the mass mission."

"I would certainly look forward to that."

This went on for another ten or so minutes. "Anything else?" Hallstatt asked. "Gorsky? Kléber?" Both of the Majors said that their questions had been answered. "All right. MacDonald, I'm going to have a quick debrief with my people, here, and I'll get back with you ... probably within the hour. Thanks for talking with us."

MacDonald dropped off. "So?" the General said. "You know, of course, that he doesn't really talk like that. In real life? That's interview-speak. He and I got past that, last night, and he's an actual human."

"Yeah," Kléber said. "I assumed he was being formal. And I say, yes, we want him. I like that *mass mission* thing."

Gorsky nodded. "Me, too. He was ready for the no-micro-management question. And he'd be really good, talking with Klein's ER bigshots."

"Okay, then. You just bought yourselves a new boss. We probably won't be able to get him onboard as fast as you did with your new Major. But quick enough. I already know who I'm going to suggest as a replacement for him. Oh, and Gorsky?"

"Yes, sir?"

"We're chewing on that little issue you brought up. There's an idea ... fermenting. I'll get back with you, or O'Neill will."

===

Alistair Felix interlaced his fingers, almost as in prayer. In fact, they were just cold. He'd gone outside, into the afternoon air, to make a call. He knew enough about the PR's surveillance capabilities to feel secure in the security of his Council-specification phone, but inside the Council Building, he was oddly wary of plain old speech. Speech could, of course, be overheard. So he went outside to speak with someone.

And the speech that had just concluded called for wariness. Prompted by — in fact almost scripted by — Newhouse and O'Neill, he'd explained to an official of some kind in the US that the PR suspected a border breach, launched by disgruntled US civilians and directed at a specific point on the Indiana border. He hinted at the freeway ransom scheme. And he hinted that the Republic was quietly preparing a reception. The other party expressed surprise, shock, dismay. She denied any US knowledge or involvement, but assured him that the US respected the Republic's right to defend itself.

"And," she'd added, "I believe we can orchestrate a response of our own. Perhaps timed to coincide with yours. So that those who might be able to withdraw back across the border wouldn't escape the claws of justice."

Or words to that effect, Felix thought. He rubbed his hands again, then called O'Neill, naming the person he'd talked to."

===

"Have you heard anything from Hallstatt?" Jeri Klein and Gorsky were comparing notes on the day's progress. There hadn't been much.

"He's doing something. And O'Neill's involved, too. But that's all I know."

"Well, it's not as if I didn't have anything else to do. The Department has another meeting with the US, up in Ottawa. Next week. And I get to answer all kinds of unanswerable questions. As per usual."

"Anything we can help with? Beyond what we're doing now?"

"I don't think so. I'm getting hourly updates from the sources you have in place, as it is, and it really doesn't look like much has changed. We'll ask for guarantees they can't give, and they'll offer aid we don't need ... eventually, the needle will stop swinging back and forth, and we'll find ..." Gorsky's phone went off. "I'll go," Klein said. "Talk to you tomorrow."

"All right." She looked at the phone display, then answered it. "Good afternoon. Could you hold briefly, please?" Klein went out and closed the door. "I'm sorry, Mister O'Neill, I was with someone. We're clear now."

She spent the next ten minutes listening, mostly. O'Neill summarized the information from Felix, attributing it to "presumably reliable sources," not to Felix by name. He had no reason to distrust Gorsky, but the fewer people who knew that a Council member was chatting with US authorities on the side, the better. He did provide the name of the US contact, and asked E to see if such a person actually existed. If so, who were they? What did they do for a living? And, if called upon to decide, would she, Gorsky, want them to marry her sister? If she had a sister. And, please, to treat this as a matter of substantial priority.

"All right," Gorsky said." I have a Sergeant on my SB team who can look at the ... person ... for us. He's not involved in the other US work we're doing ... related to the diplomatic contacts. I'd think we want those two areas kept at arm's length?" O'Neill agreed completely with that.

"For one thing," he said, "if we do keep them apart, and yet our people hear about it during the negotiations, then we'll have a measure of how widely it's known down there. Thank you very much, as always. And congratulations on having a Colonel, again."

Deeper into the mud, she thought. *And he didn't ask about satellite visuals. I think I'll just dial that up, on my own initiative.* She picked up her phone again. Shortly, the whole border with Indiana became a much more detailed subject of orbital snooping than it had been already.

=====

Colonel John Lamoreaux, head of the Republic's Field Branch, Second Division, had a substantial weapon in his care. Each of his Brigades was trained to carry out combined arms action. That was not a new idea; it meant, essentially, bringing a range of weapons and methods to bear on the opposition, together in time, not one at a time. Imagine a slapstick comedy; one person hits another with a pie, then someone else hits that person with a washtub of soapy water, and then a third actor shoves them backwards over a fourth stooge who's on all fours behind. That's *supporting* arms. *Combined* arms has all those things happening at once.

That, of course, requires training, since, for example, the kneeling comedian might well get the soapy water, too. The Republic trained extensively to avoid that, just as it trained extensively to avoid having to bring any kind of lethal force to bear on anybody. Lamoreaux and his superior, General Kydo, were talking about exactly that: keeping the event from becoming lethal.

"We don't think," she said, "that these people will be either well-armed or well-trained. The attack that we think might happen is insane. It makes no sense. But that, of course, is the problem. Your people might receive incoming fire, at least initially. Until the opposition realizes what they're up against."

"That's why I want to have our armor down there. If all they have is small arms, we can get close and talk to 'em. They can shoot their macho assault rifles at our vehicles all they want."

"We don't know, however, what else they might have. Improvised weapons like gasoline bombs can't be ruled out."

"Right. But they have to get close enough to throw 'em. What I'd worry about is if they stay in the woods. Then, we'll just have to starve 'em out."

"Very well. I'm sorry that I can't give you a place or time, yet. Or be sure it'll in Second Division. Or happen at all. So just set up a training exercise. With the little we know, we can't even assume one place. So flexibility is crucial."

"That's all right, though. It works with the training story. I'll explain it as responding to a warning order, no details ... can I say it'll be a border breach, at least?"

"There's no indication of anything starting internally."

===

Dinner time at MacDonald's house was usually a time for casual talk; serious things were typically held for the morning, so that anything that needed to be done had a whole day ahead of it. But tonight, Steve had reasons for putting some news on the table. His partner and daughter could usually read him like a book, and they were sure he had something to say. The girl's name was Angie. "Dad," she said. "How was work today?"

Twenty minutes later, Angie and her mother knew that Steve had a new job. They knew it wasn't in Bay City. And they knew they both needed to start the traditional military project of moving to a new place. Steve's wife, Aaditri, was fine with the change, and Angie was delighted. "The Capital! Wow!" was her reaction.

===

The evening wound down. Meg sat for a while at her table, now playing its desk role, reading. At 2000 hours, she put a marker in the book. The Capital was a used book gold mine, with some kind of shop in almost every neighborhood, and she'd picked up this volume on the way home from work. Now, instead of putting it on her packed bookshelf, she set it on the side table by the bed.

She undressed, put on the long T-shirt that served as a nightgown, and did her evening face-wash and tooth-brushing routine. She turned off all the lights except the one clipped to the headboard, slipped under the covers, and picked up the book. It was a textbook, written for the final year of the general education level, intended for students in their late teens. The title was *Human Sexuality in a Genderblind Society.*

===

Friday

Gorski woke up. The sun shone in their east window; Kristin was fond of raising the blinds when she got up. E could hear coffee sounds from the kitchen, along with the national news broadcast, unintelligible at this distance but unmistakable in its measured and sober tones. *We're reviving the old BBC*, she thought. *The way it used to be.*

Kristin came in. She gestured over her shoulder. "Coffee's in process. Were you thinking of getting up, at all?"

"Thinking of it, yes. Planning first, you know. Damn this 'bias for action' stuff." One of the Department of Education's dimmer managers had stumbled across that old meme, and Kristin was having a lot of fun with it. Gorski was thinking of springing it on her team, just to see who caught on to the joke. She sighed and stretched, then got one leg at a time out from under the covers. "See? Action."

===

Colonel Lamoreaux stood up from his desk and stretched. Up and back, up and back. A look at his watch confirmed that it was long enough after breakfast to take a pill. The bottle in his desk drawer said LosartalPR, 50 mg. He washed one tablet down with a swig of coffee. *Hypertension, my ass*, he thought. *But I follow orders.*

He'd lost his partner two years before, and, he had to admit, his tough-guy persona had suffered. *I'm gettin' old. But they'll have to take me out of here on a stretcher. I'm not goin' peacefully.*

The screen woke up. It said, 'Jennifer Franck,' and showed a woman in her forties with a Major's red badge. "Good morning, Colonel," she said.

"Good morning, Franck. Great news. I've decided to put on a full Brigade-level alert drill. All hands repel a border intrusion. Armor, air support, and all. An' you're it."

What hath got wrote? Franck thought, misremembering the biblical text.

===

With his initial coffee finished, Otto O'Neill was assigning himself a series of to-do items before having a second cup. A random thought appeared. *The Republic runs on coffee. We should be courting Kenya, not the US.*

The first box to check was a call to Councilman Felix. The two old acquaintances spoke briefly and hung up. O'Neill wrote in his notebook, "US contact (informal) says Indiana, not Ohio. Group still forming. No clear numbers yet. Indication still just small arms, civilian vehicles. Again, sources? Not specified." He looked at it briefly, then sent nearly verbatim messages to Newhouse, Hallstatt, and ... after a moment's thought ... Gorsky.

I'm going to have to act, there, he thought. *Rank or not, we need to move forward with her.* There was a secret—the Republic's most secret of secrets—that only a very few people in government knew. And he was more and more convinced that Major Eden Bienvenue Gorsky should be among them.

But there's work to be done first. He shredded the written notebook page. His next item was "NATO2."

===

Unlike Security Branch, the Republic's field military had no Capital Division, just the eight numbered commands, deployed around the country. Its headquarters, however, was in the Capital, occupying what had been an old and dying shopping center on the east side. It was actually an ideal position; its largely unused parking lot was repurposed for rotary wing aircraft, and it was located right at an entrance to PR23, the east side's primary north/south highway. Just to the south there was PR94, an east/west route, and PR12, an older two-lane road that ran diagonally from the eastern border in Detroit to the western corner at Lake Michigan. From there, General Kydo could travel efficiently by one means or another anywhere in the country. And it was large enough, especially in terms of single-story, ex-retail buildings, to provide housing as well as administrative space. Kydo herself had a residence there. Her mother was in questionable health, and the General's office was in the same building as the apartment the two women shared.

When Kydo was in residence, not "wandering" — as her mother put it — around the Republic, she started her working day at the breakfast table, dealing with administrative, non-classified tasks. It allowed her to spend the time with her sole remaining family member.

This morning her mother had been quiet, thinking and looking out a window. Now she said, out of nowhere, "Do you miss Egypt?"

"Egypt? I don't remember Egypt. I was three years old when we left."

"Oh, Yes. That's right. I was just thinking." There was a pause. "I miss the sun. And the heat. And people."

"We have lots of people here. All around us."

"Yes. Your soldiers. I know."

Kydo looked up from what she was doing. A sentry walked by the window. "Out on the street ... out there ... all those people going to the highway, coming in from around here to work, making the country run ... that's who we have to remember."

"I know. You have to take care of them. But ... I always thought ... there'd be a grandchild."

"Are you lonely? Is that it?"

"Yes."

"Well ... Mother, I am too. I don't need a man or ... a child. I'd like a friend, though."

"So would I. Maybe I'll get a cat."

For the first time that day ... in fact, for quite a while ... the General smiled. "And when I'm done with all of this, I'll get a dog."

===

"You know, Rich ... don't take this the wrong way. Lou thinks we should talk about who's in charge."

"Funny. I was just goin' to say that. It ain't me. I know how to do things, how to get people involved. But I'm not runnin' this."

"Oh. Okay. That's ... good. So you don't mind if ..."

"If Lou takes charge? Hell, no. I'll tell him, myself. And how about Doug? He should be helpin' out, too."

"Yeah. I guess so. Yeah, makes sense."

"Can we get 'em together? An' talk about it? They know the people, they know the country down here. People wouldn't take orders from me, if I wanted to. Give orders."

"Okay, all right. Want to meet at the Tap, again?"

"Sure. Let's get it done." The other man got up and went outside, presumably to make calls. 'Rich' rubbed his forehead. *About time.*

===

In Gorsky's Brigade area, the people specializing in imagery were busy. Meg, who was primarily a text intercept analyst, was brought into the group. "So the task here is really geography-to-text. You see images and the system's best guess at what they mean, and you use these ..." Sharon Christopher indicated a series of icons on the right side of the image area "... to get better guesses." The icons were things like a vehicle, two human symbols, two tent-like things, and so on.

"What are the tents?"

"It's asking the system to look at the imagery — the place you selected — and see if it might be a camp of some kind."

"And the people?"

"Same idea. It's people, but what are they ... *doing*, I suppose. In formation? Spread out? Building something? There's a huge library of known images, and the system tries to look at ... Yes?" Another tech, this one in uniform, had a question. "I'll be back. Keep playing with these ... " she waved at the screen "... and see if you can make sense out of it." Meg noticed that a box labeled "Location" said "Steerling IN."

===

"NATO2. What, in fact, is it?" The person presenting was one of External Relations' economic analysts. "First of all, those of you with military backgrounds may find it easy to confuse with the North Atlantic Treaty Organization. After the withdrawal of the United Kingdom and the United States, NATO became the EDO — the European Defense Organization, and it concerns itself with the security of its member nations. NATO2 — The North Atlantic *Trade* Organization — as proposed, is *not* a military structure, but a hypothetical transatlantic economic alliance. It attempts to, in effect, expand the European Union to include specific nation-states in North and South America." She paused to take a breath.

"To date, Canada is the only non-European nation that has begun negotiations with regard to NATO2. Since Canada is the Republic's sole important partner, we are compelled to remain aware of events, both as they may affect our ally, and in the more remote context of an eventual Peninsular Republic participation, on its own account. Naturally, given that the new administration in the United States is attempting to return that country's diplomatic and trade philosophy to a more global point of view, that country is also interested in following the progress of NATO2, especially as it may involve its two northern neighbors."

The audience, being well aware of all of this, had no questions. The host, representing the Republic's Council External Relations Committee, thanked the Speaker, and the conference moved on to more internal considerations.

===

This little dump, Allen thought. *Get me out of here.* His enthusiasm for the Hall's Lake Tap, never especially high, was sliding away. He was there with Doug and Lou, both large examples of white, lower-middle-class, twenty-first-century American men. They had a high school education, each, Doug had a wife and a daughter, Lou used to have a wife, and someone, identity uncertain, had given that woman a pregnancy. Each man owned — or more accurately, was making payments on —

a large pickup truck. And they both had at least one expensive, fragile, semi-automatic assault rifle.

"Now, you're not leavin' on us, are you? You're gonna be around for the ... thing?" Lou was willing enough to take on some aspects of leadership, but had just enough insight to worry about it, too.

"I'm not leavin'. But you and Doug need to lead it. The guys'll follow you two. All I'm good for is suggestin' things and pointin' things out. And we're gettin' close."

"Yeah," Doug said. "We should be puttin' a mark on the calendar soon. Some of the guys need a deadline to get 'em up off their asses and doin' some preparation." He pronounced it with the accent on the first syllable.

"Right. And like I said, they'll hear that from you. You need to be out in front."

"And another thing. So far, all we got planned is the gettin' there part. Cross the highway, cross the border, set up in that farm ... then what?" Again, Doug wanted a little more guidance."

"Rich and I talked about it, some." Lou dug out his phone. "Here's the farm." He pointed to a set of tiny marks in a cleared area, showing up on a satellite image from the Internet. "See how it's all wooded in, trees all round it? And then off to the west, there's this finger of woods? So we roll in, secure the farm, and then get people out around the edges. North, south, an' east. And on the west, we have five or six guys all the way around those woods. So they can see any trouble comin' from that way."

"And that'll take a while, trouble comin', I mean," Rich said. "Won't happen for a day, two-three days, a week ... all their ... army, I guess they call it, it's all up north of there. It'll take 'em a while to do anything. If they do."

"See, that's how this should be workin'. We get Rich's advice, and we put it in the field." Lou was getting into the spirit of command.

"Exactly. And the way to get this stuff around is word of mouth. Drop in on the guys, give 'em the word, ask 'em to pass it on. Don't do anything on the phone. That's dangerous."

"Okay, then," Doug agreed. "Let's get workin' on it."

===

Meg got to the restaurant first. It was in the middle of the old downtown, off to the west of the commercial city. The host greeted her. "Good evening. Are you dining with someone?"

"Yes, I am ... " She looked around. It was a small enough room; no sign of Larry, yet. "I think I've beaten him here. There's just the two of us."

"Fine. If you'd like to follow me ...?" She chose a table at the back wall, and took the seat looking toward the door. "I'll send your waiter over. Enjoy your meal."

She looked around. No one seemed familiar; not that it mattered, but she'd rather not have people dropping by to say hello; not this particular evening, anyway. Directly ahead, there was a woman seated by herself, with her back to Meg.

The waiter came by, noted two menus, and said, "Would you like a drink while you wait for the rest of your party?"

"No, thanks. I'll see what he wants." She glanced at the menu. "I understand the Bolognese is ... appreciated, here. Is that right?" He assured her that it was very popular.

It was only another two or three minutes before she saw Larry come in. He said something to the host, and was immediately directed toward Meg's table. *I wonder how he described me?* she thought. She noticed the host catching the waiter's eye, then pointing at Larry as he crossed the room.

"Sorry I'm late."

"You're not. I just sat down."

"Oh, good. There's a crowd out there. Must be a new film at the auditorium."

These pleasantries went on until the meal had been ordered. Two glasses of wine arrived; after a sip each, there was a shift from the trivial to the somewhat less so, essentially the *how was your day?* narrative. Meg got the question in first, and Larry talked briefly about his work. His career was in the Social Services group, looking after young people who were in one way or another adrift. Meg knew this, of course, since she'd been one of his rescues. That was not, for obvious reasons, something they'd relived during their two lunches' worth of relationship to date.

He finished a story of working with a young man who was spending excessive time creating fan art; Larry was redirecting him to writing underlying stories, instead. "You know," he began a new sentence, "I think about that sort of thing, and I sometimes remember how that wasn't like you ... how you just dug in and got yourself ... going. Without, really, a lot of help."

"Oh, I had help," she said. "You got me out of that ... away from home. And into Karen's house. That was help."

"Well, I thought it was the only thing. Really. And you just decided ... "

"I did. It was lifesaving. I learned to decide. You helped with that."

"Good. Great. Thanks for ... saying that."

There was a pause as the meals arrived. After they commented on tastes and smells and the match with the wine, there was a mildly awkward gap. Larry remembered where they'd left off, and said, "How about *your* week?"

"It's been interesting. Monday, right off, our boss got promoted. And we're a Brigade, now. The Security Branch part of us."

"Wow."

"And I think I mentioned that I'm almost done with my National Service, and I want to stay on with the group?"

"You did, yes."

"It turns out that External Relations—that's the department I work for, technically—doesn't have a position for me, full time. But the Security Branch part does. So I'm going be a cop."

"Really?"

"In name. I'll do the same things. And I'll get paid more. I get to wear a uniform. During work."

"Well ... good. Good. If you like what the job is, good. And you'll be here, still? In town?"

"Yes. Same office, same desk. Same job. But really part of the organization, not just a two-year intern."

"I didn't think I knew anybody in Security. Now I do."

"And there was another thing. Another thing I did." She took another sip of wine.

"Oh?"

"I started taking contraceptives again." She looked him directly in the eyes as she said it. Because of that, she didn't notice the reaction of the woman at the next table. It wasn't excessive, just a twitch of the head.

"I ... didn't know ... you didn't, I guess."

"Larry, remember what kind of a state I was in? Sick of school? Furious about my family? Just ... angry."

"Yes."

"And then Una got hurt. And I took care of her?"

"Yes."

"That didn't leave me with a very ... good feeling about people and men and boys. And before that, there was all the religious stuff." She paused, then with that same fierce eye contact, said, "I've never really found sex all that interesting." The woman at the next table had her head turned just enough that someone uninvolved with the conversation would have interpreted it as indicating a substantial level of prurient interest.

Larry had not expected the dinner conversation to take this turn. He'd admitted to himself, just that morning, that he was feeling things about Meg that weren't the same ones as, for example, the day before. Or five years ago. That was good, of course. Any time much before the current moment, *any* interest in her except for her general welfare would have been unethical. He took a breath. "I ... I'm sorry. I really didn't ..."

"Don't be sorry. Not at all. It's taken me a long time to calm down and get ahold of myself. And I wouldn't want you to act ... at all, in any way ... without knowing that. She stopped short, then smiled wickedly. "Get ahold of myself. Tee hee." The woman at the next table was staring straight ahead.

"So," Meg went on, "we have some choices to make. Cascading choices."

"I guess so."

"We could finish dinner and just go home. Separately. Or, we could go home together, and then we'd have to choose whose home. And regardless, there'd be other choices. Tactical ones."

"Tactical?" Larry was beginning to recover his grasp on reality. "You're starting to talk like a soldier, already."

"I'm not technically a soldier, but okay. So ... before we get too deep into the decision tree, what sounds good?"

"Together. And my place is nearer."

"Done." She waved at the waiter.

As they walked out, the woman watched them, not yet touching each other, just leaving together. *These kids, today!* she thought.

Saturday

Meg half-woke. Her body was transmitting conflicting signals. Her right arm and most of her torso were warm. Her left arm and left side were not. The room was dark, with just stripes of artificial light coming through a mostly-closed window blind. She realized that only sixty or seventy percent of her was under a sheet and blanket. Simultaneously, she remembered where she was and that she wasn't there alone. Immediately after that, she remembered that she wasn't wearing anything and neither was the person next to her.

She rolled toward him and jostled him slightly. "Hmmm?" he said.

"You're hogging the covers, sweetheart."

"Mmm. Oh. Sorry." There was a short struggle with the blankets, and equity was achieved. "Better?"

"Better," she said. "What time is it?"

"Ahh ... " There was fumbling. "6.43."

"Good. We don't have to get up. Or make any real decisions."

"Decisions?"

"Strategic ones," she yawned. "Excuse me. Long term. Like breakfast."

"Oh. Right." He was now awake, too, mostly. "How do you ... feel?"

"I'm fine."

"Really?"

"Yes. Really."

===

O'Neill was awake early. He'd gotten into the habit of thinking and writing for twenty minutes or half an hour, immediately after getting out of bed. What the subject might be was less important to him than just the doing of it. This particular morning, he was making notes—notes he would certainly destroy as soon as he'd finished them—regarding the Ability.

"The reason that the Republic exists was our demonstration of the Ability. US military forces that were sent against us were paralyzed. And later we retaliated with it against their then President as a reminder not to interfere with us. How is that different from the Intelligence gathering effort? The Ability requires information to localize its effects and to assure its harmlessness for things other than its target. It prevents coordinated action against us, just as Intelligence can do. And the measurement and analysis of its effect is best carried out with Intelligence-gathering techniques, just as it can suggest new techniques. The two are children of Attack and Defense and the parents of Safety and Comfort. We must introduce them to each other. This line of reasoning convinces me that our gradually maturing Intelligence effort should be introduced to its sibling. I propose that Major Eden Gorsky, PhD, be briefed on the Ability."

His idea of "notes" was, obviously more formal than most people's, but the purpose was the same. Writing down the arguments for something made it easier to frame them coherently when he presented them to others. He read it over twice, then slipped the page into his cross-cut shredder.

===

Bang on the dot of 0800 hours, Second Division's First Brigade command was present in the Divisional briefing room. Its commander, Major Jennifer Franck, was at the table, front and center, sharing it with Colonel Lamoreaux. All three of the Company heads were present, along with the Division's Armor commander. The Medical Officer was there, as were the Division's Security Branch and Army Air Command liaison officers.

"Good morning," said Lamoreaux. "This is a simulated threat response training exercise briefing. I'm sure all you are more comfortable with its acronym, but I'm not. So we're just going to refer to it as TX1—this year's first Brigade level training exercise. Major?"

"Yes, sir. As the Colonel explained it to me yesterday, we will be simulating a response to a reported incursion across a land border. Specifically, it is an imagined attempt by a civilian group to break in from the south and seize and occupy a small foothold within the Republic." People were taking notes.

"Some of the simulated conditions are, one, the likelihood of an incursion is known to us beforehand, but not the location. Some hours before the incursion, we will know the location and be able to prepare a response and take up defensive positions. Two, the exact time of the border crossing is not known to us. Three, the size and professionality of the opposing force is not known with certainty. Four, the opposing force is assumed not to have other than civilian small arms and heavyweight civilian vehicles.

"Our objectives are to force the opposition to surrender or retreat back south across the border. We will prefer to avoid casualties on both sides, but will return any incoming fire. We will not, regardless of circumstances, cross the border into the US, in pursuit or otherwise. We will not direct any fire such that persons or property in the US may be struck.

"Per standard procedure, non-lethal ammunition will be used during the exercise, but lethal ammunition will be carried as well." She looked over the assembled team. "The organization I have specified in response to this exercise is as follows." A chart appeared on a large screen.

"I will be in command of the Brigade and attached units. All three Companies will participate, and will act under coordination from agreed-upon plans and ad hoc orders. Command will try, given the location of the target area, to bring Companies onto the field by separate routes. Armor will be attached to one company, to be determined when the target is located. Armor will, however, be under Brigade command. Air support, in the form of intelligence gathering and target indicating aircraft, as well as casualty evacuation craft, with also act under Brigade. Aircraft will not engage in air-to-ground fire. And the usual Security Branch squad level team will be attached. A first level Medical unit will be attached, and it will locate at the direction of Brigade."

She paused and made eye contact with her Company commanders. "Questions?" she said.

===

Not surprisingly, Gorsky's "Brigade" was working over the weekend, at least in a sense. Many, many intelligence activities had been kicked off or just left running at end-of-day Friday. The people responsible for them and their output were either present or they were receiving simple "still running, nothing to report" messages on their SB phones. Meg, having just been pulled into the activity, was not on that kind of tether.

She and Larry made a toast-and-coffee breakfast at the apartment. They'd dressed casually. Meg, for example, was wearing Larry's bathrobe. "What then, Ms. Cordell, would you like to do now?" Larry asked.

"I was just thinking about that. And about a flaw in my planning."

"Flaw?"

"Yes, I heard something once ... oh, from a roommate, I guess. About always taking spare underwear along on a date. But I didn't remember to do that. So it would be nice if we could at least drop in at my place."

"That would be fine. I have to admit, I don't actually know where you live."

"Over east. It's just a tram ride. It's very, very small. The apartment, I mean."

"Great. And you know, there's a café out that way that I like. We could have something slightly more ... elaborate." He gestured at a plate, now empty except for toast crumbs.

"Good. And I have a thought, for later. Several, actually, but specifically one about sending Una ... a text, maybe. Or maybe a picture."

He looked blank, just for a moment. Then: "Ah. I see. Kind of a ... status report?"

"Yes, exactly."

===

"Let's see if Gorsky wants to join." Kléber had Major Matthews with her. The topic was the new Colonel's phrase, *mass mission*. In Kléber's opinion there were inefficiencies in the regular policing work of the Division, things that weren't contributing to what MacDonald had called "the day to day enforcement of the laws in the country's largest city." She sent a message, got no immediate reply, and said, "Let's go ahead. We can pull her in later."

"Fine." Matthews was loath to spend a great deal of time on any individual task right now, given the vast number of things in total that had to be done for her new command. "Based on what my Captains tell me, the big winners are B and E, vandalism, public intox, and a lesser amount of plain old assault. Is that what you see?"

"Well, it is, by the numbers. But what I didn't realize until I had to wear both the First and Second Brigade hats was that Second seems to have specialized in that stuff. First does some of that, but somehow, we get the outliers, too. Anything like white collar misbehavior, other kinds of fraud, misappropriation of anything ... "

"Really? That's not official, is it? Not defined?"

"No. It just somehow evolved. I went looking for that sort of order or policy ... *who you gonna call?*... stuff. Nothing. But still, if somebody's budget disappears, for example, First seems to get the job."

"My guess is that our new boss won't be thrilled with that." All three of the Brigade Majors had spoken with MacDonald, shortly after his appointment, and he'd used that *mass mission* phrase again.

"*I'm* not thrilled with it. It screws up succession plans, for one thing. No offence, but if I were short a Captain, I'm not sure if I could just bring one of your Lieutenants, say, on board. Not as an instant fit, anyway. And one of ours might not be crazy about moving to Second."

"I don't know them well enough to say, yet, but it makes sense. Question is, can we do anything about it quickly?"

"Nope. But we can document it and come up with a framework for changing it. That would at least demonstrate that we were listening. Oh, and even crazier, the Brigade command used to have specific department liaison assignments. I was Ms. Department of Education. There were days when I had no clue what else my Brigade was doing."

"What happened with that?"

"The reorganization last year cut that short. The Departments still have points-of-contact people, but they're Sergeants or Lieutenants, not Brigade heads."

"Man, that's another thing I need to know. Do I have any of those?"

"Fewer than First Brigade. And that just demonstrates the problem, again. First has DoE, Finance and Revenue, Health ... it goes on. But, sadly, I can't just rattle off yours. I'd have to look it up. And if someone from one of your Departments got through to us, we probably wouldn't be able to point 'em in the right direction."

"So ... mass mission, eh?"

"Right. I think we have to be able to pitch something to MacDonald when he gets here, even if it isn't what he has in mind. At least we'll get points for effort."

"What about Third?"

"I don't think that's the same category. They share people with ER, after all. And ER's the only customer. Well, SB in general is a customer, too. In fact, AoR as a whole, I guess. I wish Gorsky had been able to join us. I realize I don't understand her world as much as I thought I did."

"She says you helped create it."

"That was then, this is now."

===

The conversation was finally addressing the specifics. Allen — "Rich" — was finally, remotely, beginning to believe that these rustics might get around to doing something.

"Are we there, yet?" Doug's question was in reference to preparation, not arrival. "How many guys are signed up?"

"Fifty-eight. Countin' us," Lou said.

"And gear?"

"Everybody's armed up. We had to find a few loaners, you know, to keep the ammunition the same."

"Once we're in ... in and set up," said Allen, "... we'll have to look at resupply. So, keep remindin' people not to go nuts with it. I mean, best case, we don't fire a shot."

"They've been told. Some of 'em are ... kind of frisky, that way. So we're all there, out at Fredrickson's place. We go out his west side, by the barn, there." Rich and Lou nodded. "And north. Then right over to 1050. Then north again, straight up to the highway."

"Yup."

"And we make sure the trucks with blades are first," Allen added.

"Yeah. And then straight on, to the border road."

"Then left to where it curves north again. Through the fence and on up to the ... area." Lou was reciting from memory. "Then we set up, put some guards out. And in the morning, we start makin' our ... what'd you call it?"

"The approach path," said Allen. "Through the woods, back down to the border. There's a dirt track down there, on the US side."

"And down at the end of that," said Lou, "somebody's started that bridge we talked about. Across the river. So right away, we start fixin' that up. So we can get down to the interstate an' back, all in the woods."

"And we're not shuttin' the toll road down, now, to get across, right? We dropped that?"

"Right. The way we're doin' it now, we're goin' under it. On 1050 road."

"Well, hell. Let's do it. Monday night?"

"Monday night, Tuesday morning, really. Leave around, say, three AM."

"Done."

'Done' is the right word, you silly bastard, Allen thought.

===

It was yet another video call; this time it was just Hallstatt and MacDonald, working through the what and when of a new command assignment. "You've done this, as a Major, a couple of times," Hallstatt said. "This is really just a bigger scale, not really different."

"Yes and no. I was thinking through it last night, and I posed the question, *What if it was Third Division? What would I be preparing to do, if I were taking over Third?* And the answer seemed to be, spreading the workload."

"As in your *mass mission* concept?"

"Yes. Third definitely needs that kind of integration. I don't know Capital well enough, yet, to say. So that would really be my first question. To ask myself. Does the work need to be equalized? Is one Brigade good at one thing and the other one better at something else?"

"Okay. I see that. And unfortunately, I can't give you a pat answer. Colonel Achebe did a good job, but that was almost all before the reorganization. And I don't actually know how far that stuff got down into the Brigades. So, good, that's a place to start."

"I think I can merge that with the usual things—as you said, the same questions I'd ask about a Brigade. Headcount, open slots, budget adherence, morale ... all of that. Because those things will all bear on mass mission. If there's a morale issue, is it because some area is overworked and someone else isn't?"

"Right. And if Company X is always over its training budget, is it because they get all the bad jobs, and their people keep transferring out? And you know, I bet you won't get much pushback on any of that. Kléber is top notch. And Matthews is new enough that she won't have a lot of irons in the fire. I mean, inertia."

"Inertia. Exactly. That's the issue. How happy are people with the way things are? And what will it take to make them happier enough not to drag their organizational feet?"

"You know, MacDonald, sometimes it occurs to me ... this is heresy, I realize ... but minus the profit motive, this isn't really any different from running a business."

"I know. I even catch myself making up catchy names for things. Mass mission, for example."

===

Una Gregory was an old friend of Meg's and an acquaintance of Larry. Una had been Meg's roommate at Karen's House, and the two of them had been together when Una was attacked by a distraught, schizophrenic young man, off his medications, and acting as another personality. For two years, Meg had nursed Una through the physical and psychological aftermath of that experience, and she'd been the one to set up a call with the attacker, then back in a hospital and back on his meds. In that role, he, David, had been able to apologize for what "Elijah", the other personality, had done. That interaction had finally laid the ghost of Una's injuries.

Now, she was finishing her National Service in a Department of Education campus in another city. She was by herself at the moment, since her intended partner was doing forestry research, far up north. She'd had no news from Meg for a couple of weeks, and she was actually planning on a call. However, in the middle of dinner, by herself, in her apartment, she got a multimedia text from Meg. *Funny,* she thought. *She usually calls.*

What!?! The message began with a still photograph of an interior. It was obviously a bedroom, since a bed took up most of the image. There were two people in the bed, sitting up, mostly under the covers, wearing nightshirts of different kinds. They were side by side, not in contact, and both looking at the camera. They were unmistakably Meg and Larry. The text message just said, "Hi. Super busy. How's your weekend?"

===

In its lockbox, Allen's PR phone lit up. It flashed several times, and then stopped. Its noise and vibration capabilities had been turned off. The last thing Allen wanted was alerts; they might alert someone else, after all. People talked to him in his truck or leaning in a window. He'd been told, via Wickham's *alas* code word, to ignore any future messages.

Jeri Klein put her phone away. She added the date and time to a secure document, on a page labeled "Contact Attempts," typed "inactive", and closed the file. She sent Gorsky and Lorman a terse message: "Nothing."

This guy has gone deep on us. Or he's dead. She had nothing really in mind for a Saturday evening, but she still resented coming into the office, just to ping someone who wasn't pinging back. *I wonder if Gorsky's still on duty?*

Gorsky was, in fact, in the office. She and Kristin had dinner plans, but her partner was an extremely social person, and E knew she wouldn't mind if Klein joined them. There were really only a few people Kristin disliked, most of them men in her Department.

Jeri paused a second, then said, "Well, thanks. Sure. I'd like that." A few more words established a place and time. Gorsky texted Kristin about upping the reservation by one and turned back to her office machine and its budget values. *More fun than this, anyway,* she thought.

===

Meg and Larry, having sent Una their message and received a return call immediately, spent some time fielding her rather personal questions. Having established at least that their liaison was new, and that they hadn't been withholding information, they confirmed that, yes, Karen knew, and that, no, they — Meg and Larry — hadn't really talked about the future a great deal. "Seriously," Meg said, "we're just at the point of dinner options."

"I haven't even let my parents know," Larry added. "Oh, have I mentioned my parents?"

"I didn't know you had any. I thought you sprang, fully formed, from the brow of Zeus."

"No, not quite. But Dad's a bit ... doctrinaire ... I suppose the word is. Even in the PR, he's kind of a leftie." Meg had a brief vision of herself in her new uniform. She just smiled.

===

Jeri Klein, Gorski, and Kristin were seated around a window table at a downtown place, "Just Freds." Fred was not an actual person, but everyone working there had employee badges saying "Fred." Wait staff introduced themselves to customers as Fred(integer); Fred1, Fred22, and so on. There was no good reason for this. The restaurant served a modified Italian menu, and it was owned by two women, neither of whom was named Fred. That's just how the Capital's downtown was, and you either appreciated it or you didn't.

Klein knew the extent to which Kristin was not briefed — almost completely not, in fact — and it was actually a relief. To be unable to talk shop was pleasant. You could behave like ninety-eight percent of the population, and instead of concerning yourself with the safety and comfort of the masses, you could speculate about the weather, discuss film and music, and listen politely to another person talk shop and scandal about a department whose inner workings weren't a national secret.

"What happened then..." Kristin was saying, "Doctor Lange just had a fit. He's not a screamer, he just gets cold and thin-lipped and says things about being extremely disappointed. And we dumped the consultant, and the manager running the effort got reassigned to Marquette. And we won't be launching the new International Relations curriculum until next fall."

"Students won't be seeing any of the new US coverage, then?" Klein was genuinely interested. Anything about the Republic's interactions outside its borders was a professional matter for her.

"There'll be a supplement ... just a couple of days' add-ons to Second and Third Level classes. And the Fourth Level ... the degree program ... won't see anything until the full revision is out."

"I can see why he was unhappy." Mylan Lange was the head of the Department of Education. He was determined, people said, to retire with a clean record, and devil take the hindmost.

Gorsky had heard some of this before. Given what she knew about the US/PR thaw, a delay in teaching it in the schools seemed prudent. Instead of saying that, though, she steered Kristin toward another topic. Jeri looked tired, and E could easily understand it. *She's at least twenty years older than I am,* she thought. *And she's alone, as far as I know. An evening out of the trenches will be good.*

Outside, a young couple stopped to look at the posted menu. They were a bit mismatched for height, but they were holding hands and smiling at things in general. Gorsky noticed them through the window and recognized Meg Cordell. *Sharon says she's coming up to speed. I'm glad folks are getting out of the office, at least.* The two apparently didn't want what Freds had to offer, and they walked on.

"I just saw that National Service trooper of yours," E said to Klein. "The one we picked up." Jeri looked around.

"In here?"

"No, outside the window. With a friend. I assume."

"Oh, good. She seems to like doing our sort of nonsense. But at that age, you don't want to do it on an empty ... libido." Gorsky arched her eyebrows just a bit.

===

Sunday

The sun was up, but it hadn't been for long. Gorsky was up and had been for a while, back in the shop and looking at results from the satellite and communication snooping. A piece of the orbital imagery was interesting although inconclusive. Just below the border with Indiana and only a bit west of Ohio, there was a low-resolution image sequence of a place called Steerling. It was developed, but mostly around a set of lakes. South of the interstate, there was a large area of woods and open agricultural land running east to a toll plaza. Something in that greenspace had raised an imaging event, but the results were obscured by cloud cover. Because it was part of the target area she'd specified, the team had sent her the file. It was one of several others, none of which showed massive US troop concentrations, airfields packed with attack aircraft, or hordes of anything, really.

Well, hell. It's on the border. Something in the AI thought it was interesting. And there's a freeway on-ramp right there. She added it to a list of areas to be imaged again, with cloud-penetrating gear. An application showed her that a pass with advanced cameras would be five hours away. *Five hours? Hmm. Maybe we should ...*

Ten minutes after that, the SB office in the city of Coldstream, 20 K north of the border, sent a patrol car down south for a look around at the border. *Pointless, really. It's all wooded in there, and the border's 3 K north of the image site. But still ...*

===

Larry Ford woke up. There was a moment's panic, but then his hand touched Meg's shoulder. *She's here.* That was really all he needed to know, and he was prepared to go back to sleep. Meg, however, was awake too, and she rolled toward him.

"Roll over. On your right side," she said. "Away from me."

"Huh?"

"I want to see what this *spooning* thing is about."

===

"Last night's report, sir," said the Second Brigade Desk Sergeant. "Nothing on the special list."

This is like being back in Seventh, Matthews thought. *Special list?* "What's the special list?"

"It's a list of detention specifications, sir. The ones Major Wexler wanted to know about."

"There were detentions he *didn't* want to hear about?"

"Well, yes, sir. There's usually a lot of general stuff, and then the serious crimes. Homicides, weapons, large thefts, anything with injury or death. Oh, and firearms. Not many of those."

"But numbers? How many of the general things? I mean, what if there's one weapons offense and two hundred and fifty of the minor ones?"

"Those get handled, of course, sir. Specifications lodged, goes to Examination ... "

"But command didn't care if there's lots more of something, suddenly? Or fewer?"

"I'm not sure I understand, sir. Would you like to review *all* of the specifications?"

"What I want, Sergeant, is to know what's going on out there. Not just the outliers, but the ... trends. The things that might need more attention, what's declining, what's increasing? Did we get any calls here that got bumped to First Brigade because that's their world? Did they pass anything off to us? Do we really need *two* Companies? Do we need eighteen of 'em? I want the basic data so I can run the Brigade. See?" *And not to look like an idiot when my new Colonel shows up.*

"Yes, sir. I'll ... see what we'd have to do. To get you that."

"You do that. But I'll talk to the Company commanders. They're the ones who'll have to push this down. Not you.

"Yes, sir."

Matthews turned back to her screen. The first message wasn't to the Captains, though. It was to Kléber, and it was headed "Target-rich environment."

===

At their apartment, Kristin was preparing to make a particular kind of bread. Baking was a hobby, but it was becoming more of a calling. As usual, she had the Republic's National news program on, listening with half an ear as she pummeled dough.

"And now, here's Charlotte Vigan with Entertainment Updates. Charlotte?"

"Thanks, Ali. As we mentioned yesterday, The Pietrin Orkestreri will be at the National Theatre tonight, and there are still tickets available. This is a stunningly exciting concert, bringing the Finnish Saint Petersburg Orchestra to the Republic for the first time since the brief war between Finland and ..."

Kristin waved her hand at the radio, and it shut off. Neither she nor Gorsky were fond of classical music. For that evening, they had their sights on a blues band at an upstairs club in the old university district.

Their kitchen window looked out on the street, and she was momentarily distracted from kneading by the passage of an SB vehicle with its lights flashing. She frowned and started to reach for her phone. The car went by and she relaxed. From somewhere nearby, there was an actual siren. Along with the radio, there was an SB receiver that E had installed. The siren wasn't getting closer, but she turned the device on, anyway.

"... subject is running west on Huron, juvenile, probably male, carrying a ... shopping bag."

"Forty-three, is subject armed?"

"Unknown." Two other voices talked over each other. Then a new voice said, "... ject is in custody."

Kristen turned the scanner off. *Cops and robbers,* she thought. *My roommate should do something about that.*

===

Kléber and her two Captains took turns doing Sunday command. All it really meant was that one of the First Brigades' three ranking officers was there, poised to take over the response to some heinous breach of the public Safety and Comfort, when and if there was one. Usually, there wasn't.

The Republic had done what the US couldn't do, that is disarm the population. Nobody — *nobody* — but serving members of the Army of the Republic could possess a firearm and/or ammunition. It took the first five years, almost, to accomplish, but at this point it was no longer an urban problem. Out in the country, there were a few holdouts and wild asses with a weapon stashed somewhere, but they were aging (the wild asses *and* the weapons); memories were fading, and the tradeoff between stability and machismo was tilting toward the former state of mind. And of course, right after Separation, anybody who wanted to could just pack up their possessions, get a check for any real estate they might own, and head south. The US, by the terms of Separation, had to take them.

Today, the cities weren't the chaotic mess they had been. They were messy, yes, but not in the don't-walk-down-that-street-at-night way that many of them were before Separation. For example, the older towns were still transportation-messy. A standard national transport system had to be tweaked and stretched over each of them, even the ones (such as the Capital) whose street layout had roots in the nineteenth century. And the systematic seizure of land and buildings owned by organizations outside the Republic resulted in a brief housing shortage, simply because the Department of Housing had to expand its infrastructure effort every time another downtown apartment building came under their care.

By now, most of that was worked out. Radiating greenways and their accompanying tram lines—not to mention full-blown railway lines—let the cities spread as they needed to, kept down to a low roar by another national effort, a general replacement-only population policy. Finding and staying within one standard deviation from the ideal population level was one of the most-studied and most-administered efforts in the Republic. No one was forced to abandon a desire for offspring, but from their first few years in school, children heard the message; *one is enough, none is better*. It wasn't quite syntactically correct, but it was easy to say.

This morning, it was Kléber's turn to take the desk. She looked at the overnight calls and events, fifty-three of them, and saw nothing concerning. There were a few break-ins and a couple of apparently alcohol-related assaults; the rest were assorted traffic and petty theft issues. Not much for a Saturday night. *The weather mellows, and ... so do the people? That's a first.* Her experience with improving weather was that it got the extreme youth, the eighteen-year-olds fresh out of their Third Level and not yet under the thumb of Fourth Level, out on the streets and making merry. *But I'll take it,* she thought. *Now, let's have a look at the way these split up into First and Second Brigade affairs.*

===

If you stood at the north-west corner of the Capital City and launched a projectile south-east it would fly along a path dividing the town into its oldest and most heavily residential parts on your left and the newer and less random parts on the right. There would be exceptions, of course, but the old city had grown up along its river, and the river followed that same trajectory. The bulk of the modern city was south of the river, but north-east of your diagonal line.

South of your line, things became more devoted to right angles. In the newer areas, streets and roads were more likely to meet at ninety degrees. That persisted until you came to what a few sixteenth-century military architecture enthusiasts called "the city walls." Everyone else called them "the highways." A pair of highways, one north/south and one east/west, diverged and became a ring around the Capital. And they were all, to one extent or another, raised up above ground level, giving the impression of a deliberately-built set of defenses. No one had ever tested them in that role, but there they stood, enclosing the area. They weren't — perhaps unfortunately — a barrier to growth, but still, they drew a wandering line around the place, and set the area inside apart from the countryside and its *used-to-be-farms* housing developments.

Exploring this perimeter was the Sunday task Meg and Larry had set themselves. Larry did actually have a motor vehicle, seldom used but still there, dating back to a point in his career when he needed to provide occasional transportation for unhappy young people. They put together a lunch, partly from Larry's cupboard and partly from purchases on their way to a tram stop. They rode west along one of the city's four diverging east/west roads, until they were a few minutes' walk from where the car lived. They charged the battery, Meg apologized for her inability to drive — many people in the Republic grew up, lived, and died without having gotten behind a wheel — and set out to do the circumnavigation. Larry objected to that term, pointing out that a small electric car wasn't suited to any kind of navigation at all, circum or otherwise. Meg smiled and said, "Yes, dear."

They went out of the city on a north-west road, up and over one of the highways. They turned north almost as soon as they were outside the walls. It was a hilly trip, running due north and passing only small dead end roads, cut off by the highway behind them. They crossed another of the city's main entrance routes, but kept on. Larry noted that they needed further northing before they could alter course back east and still be outside the city.

Eventually, they turned east on a side road, narrow and unpaved. It led past scattered houses and woods, and it eventually brought them to the riverside and, running along it, the railroad. Just as Meg had convinced herself that they were heading back into town — and they were, technically — Larry slowed, turned north, and took them on a single-lane, wait-for-the-other-guy, bridge. There was no other guy, and they crossed. The river was in its spring high-water period, and it made a wide, blue surface. "Now we're out into the country, again," he said.

"I thought we were, already."

"We were close to civilization, back there. Now we get some more northing in." He started to say something else, but it came out as "Whoa!" He braked hard, and they watched as four whitetail deer looked up, panicked, and ran away.

===

"Sunday morning, Otto? I thought you'd be in church." General Newhouse was not in church, herself. She was up, in uniform, and in her office. And since she could see O'Neill at his desk, she knew he was on the job as well.

"No, General, I worship at the shrine of secrecy and overall sneakiness, I'm afraid. And sneakiness never sleeps."

"I thought that was rust."

"Rust may sleep, for all I know. Forgive me for interrupting your weekend chores. But I have a rare thing that I need to advocate."

"You want Gorsky be read in on the Ability."

"Yes, I do. Among the many other reasons, she's intelligent and devoted. Also, she's at least twenty years younger than a number of us. You and me, for example. We need to begin putting the next cadre of commissars into commission. Before any of us goes, gently or not, into that good night."

"I admit that I was skeptical, initially. But I remembered that I was way out of the office during the little affair up in Rainbow. And I didn't really catch on about the work she did in the Big Bay crisis until you mentioned it. But besides her, is there anyone else? I mean, that you're thinking about?"

"No. I wish there were, frankly. I see—indications—Hallstatt's new Colonel, this MacDonald fellow, may be someone to watch, possibly as a successor for Hallstatt, himself, as *he* gets on in years. But beyond that, I have no other candidates to promote."

"Well, I'm ... okay with it. I wish I knew her more closely, but I'm okay. Why don't you get the Generals and, of course, Alistair Felix together for a chat, and we'll see how they react. Hallstatt's had her reporting right to him, for what, a week or so? He'll have something to say, one way or another. And Kydo knows her from the Rainbow business. Felix, I bet, will want a full background check, which he'll ask for in the nicest, most gentlemanly way you can imagine. So let's have one in place before the meeting."

"Thank you. I will work through that with General Hallstatt." They ended the call. *That's an interesting thing there,* Otto thought. *Someone in Security Branch who needs a background investigation has it done by Security Branch. I suppose that's not a problem. I suppose.* He called Hallstatt.

===

Larry turned off their north/south road, and went east, running through woods and scattered houses. "This used to be very high-end housing, I guess." They went past a driveway with a *Department of Education* sign. "Now it's kind of a mix of co-ops and government."

Meg noticed a road sign. "That said 'Country Club Drive.' There's a golf course?"

"Used to be. I don't know anybody who plays golf anymore." They went slightly off to the south, still running through unruly, wooded land. "The river's right over there." They went on and now downhill; suddenly, there was, in fact, the river.

"So, the city's over there?"

"No, straight south, actually. My idea was to go east a bit, then north some more. So we can turn east again over the top of it. Outside the freeway ring."

"Fine." She took out her phone. "I'm going to follow on the map."

"Oh, right. I was going to suggest that." The route took them back uphill, through more ex-upscale homes, and out to a bigger, if still two-lane road. "North for a while."

Meg was alternating between the view and the dot on her phone's map. They ran north for a bit, then went east at a T intersection. The road was flat and almost exclusively wooded on each side. Ahead, though, it went sharply up. Meg glanced down at the screen. "Oh, that's the highway, right?"

"Right." They went up and quickly back down.
"So that's the north wall."

"In a way. That's part of a north/south highway that turns west when it gets to the edge of town. It'd run right down Main Street if it didn't. So we're running east along the north wall ... " He nodded toward the right. "My idea is to go on with this until we get to a southbound road. That'll take us back under the north wall and down almost to the south wall. But before that, we'll come to a nice little park. We can think about lunch."

===

"This is a new one," Matthews said. She had her phone in her hand.

"What is?" Kléber was preparing a report on equipment.

"You suggested that we might be passing certain kinds of cases from one Brigade to another? Well, it's even better than that. We're playing ping-pong."

"What?"

"This is a list of individual crime reports that have been back and forth between First and Second more than once. In the last thirty days." She sent the screen to Kléber's desktop.

"Wait. What?" She scrolled down. "Thirty-nine cases? Bucked back and forth?!"

"In a month."

"Why?!"

"That's the really interesting part. It doesn't say. There's no field for 'reason.'"

"I'm going to ... adjust my priorities. We need to appear to be dealing with this already, before we get a new Colonel in here."

"Exactly my thought. Not exactly a focus on the mass mission, is it?"

===

Lunch was the sharing out of random supplies Meg and Larry had brought or bought. The park where they stopped wasn't the oldest of the city's green spaces, but it was a well-preserved mill, dating to the nineteenth century, and it was a node on a long hiking trail throughout the south-eastern part of the Republic.

"How far around are we?" Meg asked.

"We're about halfway from where we started. Still a bit north of the river."

She was referring to her phone and its maps. "It's funny ... I've been here all this time. I never knew what it was like. Outside the city."

"I didn't really grow up here," Larry said. "But I came here for school and just never left."

"Are your parents still out there? Out west?" A small alert went off in Larry's awareness. The two of them been born in the same area, out on the lower west side of the PR. Meg was geographically and politically estranged from her parents, and Larry had lent a hand in the final, physical estrangement. "No," he said. "They retired and moved. They're up north, now. And a lot happier."

"Good." There was a pause.

"You know," Larry began, "I think we might want to formalize things. Just to the minimum necessary."

"I agree. Your place is bigger and closer to downtown, for one thing. And you're there, for another."

"So if I invited you to move in, you'd be willing to consider it?"

"Yes. I've always wanted to. For almost two days, now."

"Good. Very good. I assume, then, that's this is a kind of a love at first sight thing?"

"Maybe not first sight, exactly, but pretty near. And pretty sure."

"And you're sure pretty."

There was just a hint of a break in Meg's voice. "Flatterer."

They gathered up the remains of lunch. Meg suggested that perhaps the rest of the day would be better spent in collecting her clothing needs, toiletries, and other possessions. "It really won't take much. And then we could finish the trip around the walls next weekend."

"Fine. It actually gets a lot less interesting from here, anyway."

"And you know, my apartment's furnished. I don't have to move any furniture or anything like that. The bed's really small, but ... we could sort of pay our last respects to it. On the way out, maybe."

===

"Don't mind us. We're just collecting process data." Kléber and Matthews were standing around in the call center, waiting to watch the flow — if there was one — of assignment. The Corporal on duty did her best not to mind them, and she tried hard to remember the last time anyone over the rank of Sergeant had even been in the room. She was in charge here, with four Privates and one National Service trooper under her.

A minute or so went by. "Never a cop around when you want one," Matthews said. "Or a crime, either."

Kléber cleared her throat. It was just sufficiently spring that her allergies were waking up. "Now, in fiction, you would have just said that, and then the phone ..." A phone buzzed. "Told ya."

"Capital Division Security. What's your emergency?" One of the Privates had received the call. The officers side-stepped along the wall until they could look over his shoulder. The call information — phone and apparent location — were already in place, and the date and time were recorded. The screen also showed the nearest SB force. It was identified as Unit-2-37, a Second Brigade patrol vehicle.

"And what is the address? ... " The Private started typing. The form showed a place on South Main.

"Liquor store," Kléber said. It meant nothing to Matthews.

"And are both parties injured?" Pause. "And no one else?" Pause. "Very well, stay there. I'm sending help. I'll stay on the line as long as you ..." The *Call Ended* light came on.

"Report and hang up. Also known as *don't get involved*." Matthews knew all about that, both from her old urban assignment and the deep woods one more recently.

"Sir, it was the business at that address. The call is from their phone number." The Private was typing that into the notes section of the report.

"Okay, Private. Go ahead and do what you normally do. We're just learning."

"Yes, sir." He began clicking options. One was "DH Dispatch," the Department of Health emergency service for the Capital. The address was copied in automatically, and he clicked "Non-life-threatening assault", then added "X 2". Two subjects injured. He clicked Send.

"So there's medical help on the way now?" Kléber asked.

"Yes, sir."

"And now we do our folks? Send 2-37, whoever that is, to look for the bad guys?"

"The system does that automatically, sir. I have to confirm it, but ..." Part of the screen suddenly displayed "ADW INJ Public w INTOX rep area => 1-24."

"That means assign to a 1st Brigade unit. Unit twenty-four. It's Assault with a deadly weapon, persons injured, and in public. And some parties involved are intoxicated. It wants me to confirm that."

"But there's a Second Brigade unit closest."

The Corporal, sensing trouble, was looking at the screen, too. "Major, with a weapon and injuries, our system usually gets First Brigade to respond."

"Okay, before we hold anything up, Private ... go ahead and follow your protocol. Assign it as it says. Now, Corporal, why is that the drill?"

"I really don't know that, sir. We consulted on the design of the system ... how it works ... but the protocols are worked out between the Brigades."

"Well, well." Matthews and Kléber exchanged looks. "We're going to have to talk to the Captains, here. Or maybe even Lieutenants," Kléber said.

"Or, Lord help us, even IT."

===

Allen came back up the stairs to his small apartment. There'd been a lot of talking, a lot of pointing, all the way around the compass. Most of the pointing had been north or north-west. And the upshot of it all could be summarized as "Let's just plain do it!"

He had a party store sandwich, purchased at "The Party Store," downstairs, and a can of soda from one of the store's vending machines. His credit card still worked, but it had stopped allowing cash withdrawals. *One more night in this dump.* He put his dinner on the table, brought up the mapping software on his US phone, and began looking over the territory north of the border. Once out of the little crossroads village, it was all country, up to the interstate, then under it and on to the border. *Get over the fence, or under it, or through it ... break out my PR identification, flash it at the first cop I see ... and these guys down here can kiss my ass.*

But the problem was, if he wasn't accounted for, they might kiss off the whole thing. And the *thing* was what he'd spent nearly a year working on. Convincing a bunch — not a gang or a crew or a society, just a bunch —

of red hats that they could invade the Republic and stake a claim. And hold Interstate 80 to ransom.

Instead, what he hoped would happen — what he'd been told would happen — was that they'd be met with force in the PR and driven back over the border into forces from the US. And they'd be a huge black eye for that whole armed-high-school-dropout thing. So he was going to spend one more night here. And tomorrow night, he'd go with them, placed somehow, he hoped, so that he could slip away and turn himself in to the first PR guys he ran into.

Tomorrow. Along about, say, four in the afternoon, he'd send the alert. One word, *something*, sent to Doctor Wickham, and the troops would be waiting.

===

"So you're home." Kristin managed to make that sound warm and welcoming.

"Sorry," Gorski said. "There are all kinds of things ... not so much any one thing, just lots of little ones." This was only symbolically true. There were, in fact, lots of little things, but there was definitely one big one. Kristin either knew that or suspected it, and they had a tacit agreement that E would tell her what she could, when she could.

"Is any of that due to the new Colonel?"

"Not really. For me, anyway. Kléber and Matthews are somewhat stressed, I think. The Division seems to work all right, mostly, but they're worried about having to describe *how* it works. So they're madly finding out. And, I suppose, writing it down."

"Well, we have a new batch of bread, and if you're not heart-set on going someplace, I'll cobble things together for dinner."

"Thank you! I'm really heart-set on getting out of this uniform, into something extremely casual, and doing as little else as possible. I think I might be able to open a bottle of wine, if called upon to do so."

===

Down at the border, the Coldstream SB people were called back home. The border fence was intact, and there was nothing visibly happening on the other side. They left a video camera in place, pointed at the fence. Within a few minutes, it transmitted footage of a dog, trotting across the view from left to right.

===

Monday

A new day. A new tram ride. New work clothes. A new place. A new ... well, no, not new. A first ... love?

Meg was on her way back to work. The weekend had been different. Very different. Unlike other large changes in her life — and there had been a few — this one was startlingly positive. The phrase "It's all good" came to mind. There were decisions, of course; should they stay in Larry's apartment, or look for something else? How would they split up the household tasks? And how would they introduce each other? *This is Larry, the guy I moved in with over the weekend?* And what about a dog?

The tram slowed as three different people rang the bell. Although she'd plotted out the path to work carefully, she was still surprised at how much shorter a ride it was. *Think of the time I'll save.* She got off and walked across the open space toward the building. *I'll have something to sing about, out here. And there'll be some questions, I bet.*

===

The last thing Gorsky did before going home the day before had been to check on those satellite passes. They were scheduled, but nothing had been received. This morning, the results were in her account's inbox, in the secure area. She did a few other things first, getting the near-term, unclassified stuff off her plate. *All right, then, let's see what's up in Indiana.*

About twenty minutes later, she was typing a very classified note to General Hallstatt. "Report as of 0300 hours current day. Mixed spectrum orbital images show apparently mobile force, mixed personnel carriers and light armored vehicles, consistent with indeterminate number (3 +-) squads US Army or NatGuard infantry, located wooded area SE Steerling IN. 2k E to I-80 highway access. Ground camera at closest border road 3K north shows no activity."

To Jeri Klein, she sent a less military note. "We may have that US involvement." And then she walked out of the closed area and saw her Lieutenant talking with an analyst. She pointed a finger at him, then made the "come here" sign.

===

General Newhouse usually started the week with a headquarters staff meeting. The people she needed around her fell into a couple of categories: those who did necessary things for her, and those who kept other people away so that Newhouse could do necessary things herself. It wasn't unusual for these meetings to be interrupted, though. This morning was no exception.

"Excuse me for a minute, folks," she said. "Phil Hallstatt says he's got something important." In her office, closed up and secured, she connected with the call. "Hello, Phil. What's up?"

He told her. She listened quietly, gave it a second or so of thought, and said, "All right. *Ça commence.* I'll let Otto know, and he can tell Felix. I'll tell Kydo, and she can get Second Division poised." The call ended. *Gorsky. Just yesterday, I was fussing about briefing her on the Ability. Hell, she probably knows about it already.*

===

"Good morning, Councilmember. How are things in your world, this morning?"

"Good morning, Mister O'Neill. Things here are, as always, interesting. In fact, I was just about to call you."

"Really? Perhaps we're both concerned with the same topic. I have some news regarding our southern border. Or just short of it, actually. There appear, I'm told, to be some US forces gathering near a place called Steerling."

"Well, well, how coincidental. I was just informed, very informally, of that same thing. Not the satellite part, you understand, just the bit about troops in Steerling."

"I see. Was there anything further? Along those lines?"

"They said that Steerling was not an area of action. That was the term he used. But rather it was a gathering place, and that when the forces were deployed—his word for it, again—it would be in a line just north of the interstate and, of course, south of our border, with the line starting roughly at a point where the highway crosses a stream. The name of it is the Cub River. And he said there were orders not to advance past the border."

"Interesting. Let me just look at that ... I have it on my screen now. Where I-80 crosses the Cub River. That's ... just half a kilometer below the border. Well thank you, very much. We will treat this with extreme discretion, of course."

"I would expect nothing less of you and your people. Please enjoy the rest of your morning, O'Neill."

===

Kydo and Colonel Lamoreaux had finished their conversation. She'd asked him if he needed anything else, and he could say "no" with a clear conscience. Tactically, the ... people ... were walking or driving into trouble. He had orders for First Brigade that would bottle up the opposition, on the east, north, and west. The US, apparently, was going to shut the southern door on them. Then, they could surrender to their choice of either country, or they could just hang out in the woods until they got tired of it. The Colonel picked up his briefcase and called for his driver. *Time to go see Major Franck. All we need is a name for the opposition. Let's call 'em OpFor.*

===

It was lunchtime. Out on the courtyard, in the sunny spot they liked, Meg and her folk music friends were together. Instead of singing, though, the two SB people were interrogating Meg. "So?" one of them asked, arching her eyebrows.

"What?"

"Your date. Friday."

"Oh. It was ... fun."

"You came in this morning *singing*."

"You did," said the other one. "And then you went right to see Sharon."

Meg smiled. "Last week, you asked me if my lunch date was like 'The Maid Went to the Mill.'"

"So?"

"So this weekend was more ... *What was said or what was done, Diel confound me gin I'll tell ...*"

"But the line after that is "*Oh, I fear the country soon will ken as weel's mysel.*"

"Well, not quite the way that means. But ... anyone who can see my personnel records will *ken* that my address has changed."

The other two smiled. "Congratulations. Are you happy about it?"

"Oh, no, not at all," she said, flashing a broad, broad grin.

===

Second Division's headquarters were in the city of Grand Rapids. It was the largest city on the west side of the Republic and a regional center for government and the economy. It had been a center of resistance to Separation, having had a large population of right-inclined people, and for both practical and symbolic reasons the new nation put a garrison there. But unlike the Capital area, Second Division was a widespread region, and so its two Field Branch Brigades were split between the big city at the north end and a smaller urban area to the south. First Brigade had its home there.

The legacy freeway, PR 94, ran east/west across the Division, more or less centrally. And just south of that line, the Division's First Brigade had its headquarters near a town called Blackford. It was right at the intersection of PR 94 and another large route, PR 131, running north/south. From there, it could deploy quickly in any direction, and, at the current moment, it was about to do so.

Its First Company was packed and heading south on 131, ordered to go as far as a place called Constantine, and then east on another highway to the town of Sturman. That was just five kilometers north of the Indiana border. First Company would hold there, remaining with the vehicles and ready to move again on notice.

Second and Third Companies headed east from their base, moving in reverse order. Third Company, including four armored personnel carriers and two lighter all-wheel-drive reconnaissance vehicles — military pickup trucks — went first, followed by Second and its transport, a Field Medical Unit, and Command. *Command*, of course, meant Colonel Lamoreaux and Major Jennifer Franck.

Both Second and Third would run east on the other freeway to a point just south of an ex-industrial town called Battle Creek. Then they'd turn south on a smaller highway and carry on until they reached their waiting position, clustered around a small rural village. All three

Companies would then be less than twenty kilometers from their target areas; the orders for all of them were to hold until nightfall, then advance a small further distance into each of several deployment positions. Those positions would be just five or six hundred meters from an "objective".

The exercise was designed, Lamoreaux explained, to simulate a quick, defensive move toward the border, intended to establish a barrier against any further advance north from a border crossing. "Of course," he said, "if we really thought the US was comin' north, we'd have the whole Division down here, and First Division off to the east, and more help comin' down from the north. But this is an exercise. And so we just focus on what's in front of us. Like the Sergeant said in that old Africa movie, *because we're here, lads. Just us. Nobody else.*" It wasn't an entirely accurate quote, but he felt sure that no one listening to him would have seen the film.

===

Major Gorsky, Security Branch Capital Division, Commanding Third Brigade, wished for a window. That was not possible in any place truly secure, but still. *Something else to look at except this damn screen. It's all happening again. And this time, bloodshed. Almost guaranteed.*

The last time her new career — as a seeker of intelligence rather than a police officer — had brought her into contact with a doomed insurrection, the revolutionaries had a dozen or so pistols or hunting weapons. Now, assuming the leaks from the US were valid, there were sixty-some fools with assault rifles. Generals Kydo and Hallstatt had called her, jointly, and put her in charge of intelligence for the response.

"Expect requests from either of us," Hallstatt had said, "and maybe directly from the Colonel of Second Division. That's Johnny Lamoreaux. And until we know the OpFor ... did I say, that's what we're calling them? ... is there, for sure, nobody else knows this is live action. Everybody from Brigade command on down thinks it's a drill."

"Yes, sir," she'd said. "And will the Colonel determine when it's live? Or you, General Kydo?"

"I'll make that decision, based on your intel. Especially imagery. And I'll pass that to Colonel Lamoreaux."

"And, obviously, if OpFor opens up on our people, first." Hallstatt didn't really want to say that, but it was reality.

Sure, Gorsky thought. *One idiot shoots, the whole Brigade opens up.* "Is there a command location? Here in the Capital, I mean?"

"I'll be in my office. General Hallstatt has asked to be here, too. Anything from you will get to us on that secure link."

"And Lamoreaux will have a secure connection, too. He's got a portable with him," Hallstatt added.

"Oh," said Gorsky. "He's going to be with the Brigade, in person?"

"Yes. I should have made that clear," said Kydo.

"When this ... we need a term for real action starting ..."
"NLAD? No longer a drill?" Hallstatt wished he'd thought of that issue earlier.

"Fine. When we are NLAD, start copying that machine on anything you'd send to me. Here is the link."

Gorsky recalled a slight feeling of concern. *That sounded a bit ... ad hoc. Is there a doctrine in place for turning a training exercise into an active defense? Why would there be?*

"Do you think we should give that link—the link to the Colonel's machine—a trial? I could send some routine imagery ..."

"Is there a concern there?"

"Not specifically, but things can go wrong."

"Fine. I'll call the Colonel."

The test worked. Lamoreaux was able to see trams moving around in the Capital, directly downlinked from a geosynchronous satellite. His comment was just, "Works for me."

===

Meg stopped by the desk of her team leader. She'd noticed an increase in activity, especially among the higher-ranking people. "Is there something I can take on? It looks like people are being pulled away."

Her Corporal thought about that. "How about ... this?" She brought up an "analysis proposal," essentially a requirements document. It was from a specific group, in another Division, and it asked for length-of-trip averages on small boats leaving a specific bay on the south shore of Lake Erie.

"Somebody — somebody in Canada — thinks there could be smuggling coming out of this place. Going over to their side. So a metric ... what's a normal time on the water? For private boats. Sami can point you at some routines she's used before."

"Okay, I'll talk to her. And you'd want to look at it, right? Before I sent it?"

"Right. Have a ball."

===

Jeri Klein had, much to her displeasure, skipped a second cup of coffee. Medical advice was one thing, simply functioning was another. "If you don't sleep, you're going to regret it," the doctor had said. "Or, you won't regret it or anything else. If you follow me." But sleep had been a problem for so long that her work spilled over into the late hours. There were things she needed to do and things she believed she should be doing, even if no one really paid attention to the latter.

Now, with a headache and a general distaste for everything, she was moving printed documents around, commenting on some, just moving others. She pushed away a single page of something, and it slid to the back of the desk and onto the floor. Dammit! She started to get up, but her phone went off. Nothing. *What the hell ...? Oh!* It wasn't her phone, it was the Wickham phone, locked in her document safe. *Oh ...!* She fumbled with the lock, entering the password incorrectly once, getting it right on the second try. She pulled the door open. The phone was no longer ringing, but its red LED was blinking.

She'd changed its password to something she could remember, and now she found it hard to remember what it was. *Slow down.* She cleared her mind as much as possible; after a second, the new password popped up, visualized as the characters she'd typed as she changed it. The phone unlocked.

There was a single text message waiting. She brought it up. The first line read "SOMETHING 0300 57 18 XIT." Below it, another line said "--------- ---T --P --V -AP."
"Amateurs!" Klein said out loud. She reached for her own phone and called Gorsky."This is Klein. We got something," she said.

===

Gorsky made two calls. One was to Kydo and one to Sharon Cristopher, the lead ER analyst. That person was, of course, a few meters away, but this wasn't a good time to be away from one's desk. "I need a code-smart analyst," she said. "They don't have to be highly briefed, just able to make sense of some nonsense for me."

Christopher knew what "nonsense" meant in this context. She said, "Be right there." Shortly after, Meg was at the door to Gorsky's secure office.

===

There were two Generals, a Major, and Jeri Klein on the phone, again. They were all well-grounded in their fields, at high levels of their organizations, and were well-educated professionals. Consequently, no one said, "We've got to stop meeting like this." In fact, all four would have been happy to stop, old meme or not.

"This is what we have," said Klein. "I got a call... a text message, actually... from the individual that Wickham planted. He or somebody who knew the code word, anyway. According to Wickham, a message starting with "something" meant that the incursion was on, timed for three to four hundred hours the following day. It also had a string of letters and characters that, we assume, were details, but nothing Wickham gave us mentioned that."

"What did it say?" General Kydo was in her bird-of-prey mode, leaning forward, focused on the speaker.

Gorski answered. She was beginning to feel a bit protective of Klein. There were hints of fatigue in Jeri's voice and expression. "We gave it to one of our analysts—she's good at getting around this kind of juvenilia. I showed it to her, and she sat there in my office for about two minutes and came back with this." She put an image of a handwritten page up on the conference screen.

"That's the message content, at the top. This is what our person got out of it, verbatim."

"First word is *something*. That's nine characters and the first symbol is nine dashes. It's probably just a confirmation. *If this has the same characters as the first word, it's OK. Believe the rest of the message.* Then, there's 0300 and dash, dash, dash T. So that's probably "time". The next one would logically be date, but it doesn't work. If we're right about the first one, the dashes are digits, up to 999. So something at 0300 hours is going to be 57P. Parts, positions, people ... yeah, maybe fifty-seven people. The same with the next one. If it's digits, there's going to be eighteen V something. Fifty-seven people with ... oh, fifty-seven people in eighteen *vehicles*, maybe? And the last one, that's probably contextual. It says *XIT* ... maybe *exit?* but *AP*. I don't get that one. Somebody's initials?

"Now, this young woman is not read in on any of this. She was an intern in Doctor Klein's group for two years, and then we brought her on as a PFC on our side. That was just this week. She's going at this blind, and the only part that stumped her was the AP. That's the guy. Allen Posten. He's going to XIT."

"Make sure we retain her," said Hallstatt.

"Absolutely, sir. My only concern about her would be whether we can keep her interested."

"I'm sure we'll have more little puzzles for her," Kydo said. "So ... I will give this to our First Division."

"What are we going to tell them?" Klein was unhappy.

"That we expect to hear from them, sometime during the night, if they are seeing actual border breaches. We will likely know from satellite data before they do. Either way, they are to confirm our orders to go into combat rather than training posture, and to begin carrying out the block-and-demand-surrender plan in expectation of resistance, possibly force." The room was silent.

"What ... if ... " Klein started. Gorski stepped in.

"We don't have a choice. If nothing happens, then we got bad information. And if the US actually puts troops on their side, and nothing happens ... same thing. If there are no targets, we don't shoot. We don't even move. And if there are people, and we scare them into going back across the border, and if they run into a US force, that's their issue."

"What if it's somewhere else?"

"We've got satellites looking at every meter of the border. And they're not seeing anything that looks like even a small group. Right now, we don't even see one in the suspect area. But if we do, we can shift our focus."

Hallstatt knew Gorski less well than he wanted to. *I'll be damned,* he thought. "Yeah, true enough. I mean, our whole Indiana/Ohio border is just 280-some K. And we've got two Divisions — three more Brigades — east to west along it."

"And we've committed only a small air component to this plan. The rest are available for any other issues." Kydo was verging on grim.

"I ... all right. I see the issues. What about ... " Klein's face hardened. "What if we wake up in the morning, in bed with the US? What do we say to each other?"

Gorsky took a deep breath. "What Doctor Klein is asking about, I think, is ... a public face or, for that matter, an international face, on this event. What does Canada think about our ... allowing a US opposition group to fall into a jointly-set trap? Jointly between us and the US?"

"And even more so, not just *allowing* them. *Luring* them, is the term I'd use." Klein was grim.

"Doctor," Gorsky said, "No one on this call is responsible for that. You didn't set up Wickham's little project. I didn't. Neither SB nor FB did. But we are, all of us, required to deal with it. And we have to do it within the law. Anytime your people want to, SB can arrest Wickham and go public with the whole thing. But I don't think we want that, yet."

"Why not?"

"Because what I'd want, if I had a choice, is an example of the PR and the US cooperating to put down a dangerous plot to interrupt traffic on the Indiana Turnpike. And if I were the US, I bet that's what they'd want, too, these days."

"I agree," said Kydo.

"Ah, yes. Yes, I think that's really the ... idea." Hallstatt was simultaneously delighted with Gorsky and concerned with Klein. "And I think there's another thing. ER and a lot of departments are looking at NATO2, and we don't want to give any ... bad impressions ... there."

"All right," Klein said. "I want to see what Otto O'Neill thinks about this, first."

"We can call him," said Kydo. They did. O'Neill answered his phone quickly. The call lasted a few minutes, with Klein probing him about ramifications and considerations. He was polite, friendly, slightly formal — all the things he usually was — and ended by saying that, taken on balance, he agreed that putting First Brigade, Second Division into a defensive warning status on the Cub River was really the best action, at the moment.

===

Meg was slightly surprised by the positive feedback passed down from the Major's office, but she'd already internalized some of the subtleties involved in secure work. You could do a good job on something, but never know what the job really was or what was good about what you did. You smiled and said, "Thank you, sir."

Now, she was primarily interested in going home — "home" being Larry's apartment — and seeing what kind of dinner the two of them might put together from his meagre supply of groceries. She made a quick inventory of her shoulder bag's contents. Personal phone, department phone, apartment key card, random other contents ... she stood up, but Sharon Christopher was coming along the cubes, speaking with staff. Meg waited. Sharon's message to her was simple but interesting. "Don't be far from transport or the office itself, tonight. We might need people to come in." Meg had seen this once or twice before, and you could tell something about the issue in question from observing who went home and who stayed. This evening, the younger or newer people were heading home; the old hands were hanging on. She felt vaguely jealous.

===

The sun was down, and the light was gone. North of the Cub River, the First Brigade had reached its holding points. First Company was concealed at the edge of a large wooded area; it faced east with a view — and a field of fire — across open ground. The southern half of that view was closed off by a finger of woods running north from what had been a farm. On their tactical maps, it was marked 'Farm 2.'

Due north of the finger and going substantially further east, Second and Third Companies were set up along an east/west road. At the east end of that position, the armored vehicles were in place. To their south, the country was open, right up to Farm 2. And the border was due south of there, with nothing but open grassland in between.

The only lights to be seen were occasional glimpses of late night traffic, going east or west on the interstate highway. Half a kilometer north of First Company, Colonel Lamoreaux and Major Franck had a shared headquarters set up. The Colonel's tent was flagged as a secure area, and a pair of Privates were at the doors, enforcing that status.

Inside, Lamoreaux had a folding table and a portable device. The device was running, displaying satellite imagery. When darkness had settled in, he'd gone out, closed the tent flaps, and walked back and forth along the headquarters area, using a pair of night binoculars to look over the terrain. Not long after that, he told his staff Lieutenant that he was going inside to monitor communications.

===

Tuesday in the Dark

Monday died quietly as midnight passed. In a field just south of the interstate, pickup trucks were gathering. A few people were actively directing them into a kind of queue, others were just standing around, talking quietly. Above them, clouds drifted slowly northeast. Traffic noise from the highway was diminishing. There weren't any hills to require downshifts or acceleration or even braking, and the nearest on and off ramps were miles away. Even though diesels were still legal in the US, the truck noise was minimal.

The de facto leaders, Lou and Doug, were circulating, reviewing the basic program over and over again. At one truck they'd get quiet agreement, from another, suggested modifications, from some, just ordinary weirdness. They walked away from a standout example of that, shaking their heads. The lone occupant of a truck, a large, dark-haired woman called May, had growled and complained nonstop, unhappy with just about every aspect of the plan. "She's always got something to say," said Doug.

"I'd tell her to go the hell home, but she's a damn good shot, and she's meaner than most of these other guys," said Lou. "If we run into any crap from the cops up there, she'll be in the front line."

"Did you talk to Jimmy?"

"Yeah, I told Stu to get him a ride with Rich. He can do stuff for us, I guess."

"He's kinda the opposite of May. Quiet, no guns. But he wants to go, so what the hell."

Across the field, two figures walked up to one of the trucks. "Hey, Rich? That you? I got a passenger for ya." Stu was standing by Allen's truck, staged fifth in the convoy. Ahead were Lou and Doug's vehicles, themselves behind a pair of high-end work trucks, each one of them with a V-plow on the nose.

"This guy's goin' with us," Stu said. "He's gonna help with, you know, food and keepin' track o' things. Like that. Just drop him where Lou ends up." The person in question was obviously younger than the usual age for this bunch, and he seemed to be unarmed. Since Allen's plan was to slip away and get clear of the whole mess, this wasn't welcome, but he couldn't think of a reason to refuse.

"All right. Come on in."

He not only looked young, he sounded like it. "I'm Jimmy. I ... just want to help."

"No weapon?"

"What? Oh, no. No, I don't have a gun."

"All right. Just sit still. Put the seat belt on. And stay put until I tell you to get out."

===

Gorsky was in her office, shoes off, feet up on the desk, trying to relax. There was a great deal of nothing happening. The one known concentration of troops, other than their own, was the apparently US forces, off to the east. Nothing seemed to have changed with them. Security Branch people were keeping an orbital watch on the highway border north from there, plus the lone ground camera, but it was all quiet, the border fenced off, deserted.

Outside, in the Intel group's work area, the team was taking turns looking at things, dozing, and going back to looking at things.

Klein was also in her office, actually asleep. Every fifteen minutes, her phone would beep, prompting her to check for news. The last time, she'd slept through it.

In Kydo's headquarters, nobody was sleeping. She herself was alternating among her people, looking silently over their shoulders, then moving to someone else. This wasn't new to any of the staff. Few of them knew anything about the real situation; this was just the norm when there was any kind of Brigade or Division-level simulation going on.

Hallstatt was with Kydo, hanging out in her secure conference room, and online with General Newhouse. Both of them were dozing, waking, dozing ... *I hate these things*, he thought, during the most recent waking period.

===

At 0235 hours, Lou sat up in the cab of his truck. *Fuck it,* he said to himself. *Let's get it done.* He called a group number on his phone, said, "Let's go!" and turned the key in his ignition. Up and down the rows of trucks, engines began to start. He got a call from Doug: "We goin'?"

"Yeah. Go!" he answered.

===

In Gorsky's area, an analyst was staring at imagery from a chain of satellites, each bird handing off to the next one as it passed out of a field of interest. She suddenly sat up and tapped the person next over. "Check my math!"

"You got IR, there. Engine heat. Somebody ... wow, look at that! Lots of engines!"

"That's due south of the area!" She clicked 'Forward' on the screen. In her office, Gorsky snapped her chair back upright. *Oh, fabulous!* There was a large box on the screen labeled GROUP; she dragged the imagery feed onto it.

In Kydo's office, she and Hallstatt saw it almost simultaneously. The hot spots began to resolve themselves into a line, a line that gradually stretched out onto a road, headed north. Hallstatt acknowledged receipt, back to Gorsky. Kydo called Colonel Lamoreaux. There was no answer.

===

On Indiana N950, Lou was watching the tailgate of the truck ahead. They were running without lights, of course, but brake lights were another story. Every time anyone tapped a brake pedal, there'd be a ripple of red, running down the convoy. *Hope there's nobody watchin'.* The first turn was coming up, a right, off to the east, then a left up north to the border. *Keep it stretched out, guys*, he thought. *No tailgatin'.*

Two trucks back, Allen and his passenger were silent. They made the turn, and there was no phone chatter, so presumably the rest of the group was with them ... *or too stupid to know they're lost.* Jimmy the passenger was looking straight ahead. His right hand was clutching the arm rest, and his knuckles were white.

===

"Turning east." The comments could have been from any of the people watching the satellite data. "Where are they going? That road they were on ended. They have to turn. Maybe north on the next one ... N1000?" General Kydo was not paying attention to any of that. Instead, she was communicating with Major Franck. Franck did answer.

"This is Franck."

"Major, this is General Kydo. I am unable to contact your commander. Are you with Colonel Lamoreaux?"

"Not ... in person, sir. He's in his command tent."

"Far from you?"

"No, sir. Right here. Close."

"Go and find him. Stay in contact with me."

"Yes, sir. On my way." *What in the hell?*

Kydo was thinking as fast as she could. *I could go. Don't be ridiculous. By the time you got to a helicopter, it'd be over. I could command remotely. We know how well that works! It has to be Franck. She's on the scene. She's next in command. She ...*"

"General?"

"Yes!"

"Colonel Lamoreaux is ... unresponsive. Medical is coming. I ... think he may be dead!"

===

Not too long, now. Another couple of ... yeah, here. Allen saw the truck ahead brake, and then it turned left. An absurd thought came to him. *A left turn has to yield to oncoming traffic.* Behind him, the rest of the convoy slowed, watching the red lights ahead. Without much in the way of trouble, the invasion was halfway to its target.

===

Kydo got Gorsky and Newhouse on line. *Shall I get Klein, too? No, this is Army business.*

"I have the Commander of First Brigade, Second Division with us. Major Franck, we are live with General Newhouse, General Hallstatt, and Major Gorsky. Franck has reported to me that Colonel Lamoreaux is at least out of action. She says he may have suffered a stroke or had a heart attack. We don't know his condition. The Brigade's medical team is in charge, there. My recommendation is to brief Major Franck on the full mission and place her in local command."

There was a short pause, representing the amount of time each person took to do the same analysis of alternatives that Kydo had already done. Newhouse cut through any possible objections. "That's what succession is for. Go ahead."

"Very well. Major Franck, you are now in command of the operation. You were in command of a training exercise; it is now an actual effort to contain a genuine border breach. Is that clear?"

"I ... think so. This is a live action? Not training."

"Exactly. The term we're using is NLAD. No longer a drill."

"Weapons free? Live ammunition?"

"Yes, if you are fired upon."

"Objective?"

"As with the exercise, contain the incursion." The conversation was taking place over terminals. Kydo's phone sounded. "Excuse me." She listened for a moment. "And based on what I was just told, expect US forces to appear south of our border, also responding to the event."

Given all the other things Franck had to remember, it was five or six minutes before she thought, *who's Major Gorsky?*

===

Allen came out of the freeway underpass. They'd already gone past the only commercial enterprise on the north leg. Some kind of agricultural processing ... *thing. Plant. Or something.* The taxonomic functions in his brain were being sidelined. If a quadruped of some kind had crossed the road, he might have avoided hitting it, but identifying it as a cow or a moose would not have been given a lot of priority. "Half a klick to the highway," he said, then caught himself. "Quarter mile, I mean." *Watch your mouth! Don't blow it now!* Jimmy didn't seem to care, one way or the other. *He might not be too bright,* Allen thought.

It wasn't much of a bridge. It took the road up just far enough that commercial traffic on I-80 could reliably clear it without a disastrous, seventy-mile-an-hour collision in which, say, the shiny new vehicles on top of a car transporter were just sheared off. In a breath, they were over the interstate. Ahead, there was just one more turn, left, back west almost as far as they'd come east ... and then, *bust the fence.*

===

The Intel office was now just a larger secure area. The elevator lobby doors were locked, and nobody in the room lacked any clearances. Gorsky, phone in hand, was walking up and down the cubes, looking over shoulders at screens, pointing at things and asking questions. Some of the group disliked this level of management, others were glad to see her, ready to tell them how to react to something, relieving them of the decision.

She was looking at the line of images—not actual pictures of trucks, just rectangles, marked 'V' for vehicle. It was bent around in a right angle, with the front moving west, leading the remainder north up toward the border. "So far, Major," said the analyst whose screen it was, "they're still technically in the US. The border's right along the north edge of that road. And the fence, of course." He started to say something else, but another person, a cube or two away, said, "US movement!"

Three quick steps in that direction showed Gorsky what the woman at that machine was seeing. Dots without letters or symbols were beginning to move north-west, on a highway marked Indiana 120. "Somebody ... you, Susan, keep watching those guys! If they go north, I want to know. If they go north of the freeway, I *really* want to know."

She stepped back and raised her voice. "Good stuff! I'll be back in a minute. I have to go talk to some Generals."

===

Allen had no real way of knowing, himself, but the last of the convoy was just turning onto the western road. The name was Greenfield Road, and in another month it would live up to its name. North and south of it—and thus, north and south of the border—there would, in fact, be green fields. Right now, they were still plowed and ready to be sown with crops. *I hope it doesn't rain. Mud. Not good.* He was terrified. He was experiencing what countless soldiers had felt before him, moving relentlessly toward battle. Jimmy was staring out the right window, looking through the border fence.

Lou, with Doug behind him, saw the road make its northern turn. The pavement kept going, but the border fence simply cut it off, running on west and into the woods along the Cub River. Suddenly, there were brake lights ahead. Lou's phone buzzed.

"What?"

"We're at the fence."

"Okay. Bust it down."

"Like, one at a time? Or both at once. Both trucks?"

"You got the blades. I can't see shit, back here. Do what you gotta, just get goin'."

"Okay."

===

In her office, Gorsky was giving the assembled Generals a summary. "Any minute now, OpFor will be at their turning point. They can't keep going west, they'll run out of road. And the US ... force, or whatever it is ... should be able to be in the area in twenty minutes. If they're troop carriers. And if they get on the freeway. And if they're even coming here. Here, as in where OpFor is."

"I'm passing this to Major Franck," Kydo said. "Do we have a count, yet?"

"Of vehicles, yes. We got some magnified imagery ... " She put a vague picture of a pickup truck on the shared area. "There are eighteen of these on the road. Or similar vehicles. We're guessing forty to sixty people."

"Oh," said Hallstatt. "We may have a problem, there."

"What?" Kydo was in full awareness mode.

"When the public idea of this was a drill, First Division got a token Medical Unit assigned and a token Security Branch presence. But not scaled to sixty potential casualties. Or prisoners. And more than token air evac, as far as I know."

"Wow," Newhouse said. "Let's fix that, shall we? Kydo, you see who you can round up as medical. No, wait. You're going to have to talk Franck through this. I'll talk to the doctors. Phil, call ... who, First Division? Or Second? For uniformed cops. And I'll wake up the helicopter folks when I'm done with Medical. In fact, maybe we can have the rotaries bring in some of that advanced help, either way. SB or Med."

"General?"

"Yes, Gorsky?"

"Major Matthews — our new Second Brigade command — is on duty tonight. Is it reasonable to give her a warning order, for the Capital area?"

"For Capital ... I hadn't thought of that. Phil ...?"

"Yes. Good idea. Just a very general message, maybe. Just ... in case people call in, *no danger, no need to shelter ...* like that."

"Good. Let's do it. And I'll tell my help here to touch base with the press office. Gorsky, go ahead and to talk to ... who's the new Major?"

"Matthews, sir. I'll call her now."

"All right, let's say ... fifteen minutes away from this for, ah, Phil, Gorsky, me ... Kydo, that leaves you still on this call. Ping any of us if there's action."

===

It was warm enough. Lou had his window rolled down. Engine noise was growing as trucks came in behind. But then, things peaked. The first hit on the border fence made an incredible engine-roar-scrunch-scraping sound. *Jesus!* There was a pause, then the second blade-bearing vehicle jumped in, a little right of the other one. Again, a nasty, chaotic noise, followed by a crash. Lou's phone went off.

"They got part of it. Pole and all."

"Well, get the rest. Big enough for a truck, and nothing to get jammed up underneath!" *We should have tried this, first, somewhere!*

===

"Major! Major Franck?"

"What?"

"Some kind of noise, down south. Like a crash, or something!"

"All right. Keep me informed." She sent Kydo that information. She got back: "OpFor is likely breaking through border fence. Stand by for orders." Franck had just time to internalize that when she got another text. "What is the status of ammunition switch?"

That's a good question. All the units had the same amount of live rounds as training cartridges. But all three Companies were scrambling to get them swapped out. "In progress," she responded. "Will confirm in ten."

"Understood. Be advised additional medical units will be en route. Also SB prisoner handling aid. No ETA available yet."

Lovely. Understood.

===

"Hey, Matthews?"

"Yeah, Gorsky? You still in the shop?"

"I am. Look, I can't say much, but be aware that you might start getting ... concerned calls from ... um, concerned citizens. About things happening in Second Division. Let the desk people know that, quote, 'Field Branch is aware of issues of concern, and measures have been taken to assure security. There is no threat outside of a small area along the southern border, and only a minimal concern there.'"

"A minimal concern?"

"Yes."

"Okay. I'll pass that on. What about the press?"

"Refer them to AoR Command. The press guys there. They should know that, but sometimes the reporters do try to poke around. If you get questions from them, don't even say what I just told you. Only to, you know, individuals."

"Concerned individuals."

"Right. Welcome to the big city." Gorsky hung up. *Okay, back to ... damn!* Four minutes later, she ended a call with the satellite people, having asked them to add enhanced and ongoing surveillance of the Capital area and of the lakes. The Capital was, she was almost certain, not under any kind of threat, *but if we're telling nervous members of the public that, we'd better be sure.* And as for the water borders, *who the hell knows? But let's be sure nobody's drawn our attention to a land border, and then tries to do ... something by sea.*

===

The last mangled section of chain link fence was dragged out of the way. *Damn stuff was tougher than I thought.* Lou was only slightly concerned. They'd made a hell of a noise, over nearly fifteen minutes, and nobody even turned on a light, up north. "Okay, let's go. I'm leadin' now." He got back in his truck and started it up, pointing the vehicle through the gap in the border and on north.

Allen would have been third in line, now, after Doug, but one of the crash trucks cut in ahead. He let it. Precedence was the last thing on his mind. Two hundred and fifty meters, more or less, straight ahead, a farm and its driveway would be their destination. Behind it was a rectangle of woods, sticking up into farmed fields. The specific place where the group meant to set up headquarters was abandoned, but a bit further north, along an east/west road, there were occupied places, places where people lived and carried out farm activities on just about any land that wasn't part of a nature area and covered with woods.

Slip away, walk west through the woods. Use my phone to keep on goin' west. Surrender to the first troops I see. That was the extent of his plan. The worry was that his message about the event starting didn't seem to have brought out any troops. What he didn't know was that, yes, it had.

On the passenger's side of the truck, Jimmy was looking around. It was too dark to tell much about the land, but everything on his side was open ground. And there didn't seem to be any structures, either. No houses, barns, sheds. Just open ground. His hand was white-knuckled, still, gripping the door handle.

===

"Major Franck," Kydo said, "We see evidence that the OpFor has entered the Republic. They are advancing up Greenfield Road, still in line formation, toward your position. When satellite imagery shows that they have reached a set of buildings five hundred meters south of Second Company's position I will ... wait. Yes, Gorski?"

"OpFor has reached the farm. Position 1."

"Franck, OpFor has reached the maximum distance we intend to allow. Light up and carry out your tactical plan."

"Yes, sir," Franck said. She didn't like this, not at all. But there was nothing for it. Ten minutes ago, the medical unit had confirmed Lamoreaux's death; cause, cerebrovascular accident—a stroke. *It's just me. Nobody else.* She sent company commanders a single message: *Illuminate.* And to the Third Company, she sent *Advance Armor.*

===

Lou had just descended from his truck. "We should have half the guys pull off into that field. The one we just went by? There ain't gonna be room for all of 'em up here."

Doug was about to agree. He happened to be looking north, standing near the road with Lou. Suddenly, there was a set of small noises and flashes, all along the north boundary of his vision. "What ..." He started to say, but then the whole area lit up with a stark white light. Parachute flares began to wobble around in the sky overhead, each one blazing with LEDs.

===

"Sir, imagery is showing illumination, all along the north side of the affected area." Gorsky nodded.

"I see it." She was out in the team area. To Kydo, she sent "Illumination is visible from orbital sources." She turned back to a different cube. "Any gunfire?"

"Negative, sir. I ... Wait. Yes. Getting small arms flashes here." He pointed to the northern edge of the farm's woods. "People in there are firing."

"Okay, I'm going back in the conference room. Put stuff up on that display as it comes in." *I'm not actually going anywhere ... except my office. To look at a screen. Digital brain, here I am.*

===

Brigade Headquarters could have been better positioned. It was assumed to be an administrative function, and Captain Franck was not doing any kind of administrative work at the moment. She'd moved herself and her staff east, away from the post and to the edge of a small point of trees. From its eastern edge, she could see diagonally south into the open fields and the west side of the finger—the north/south rectangle of woods that hid the farm from First Company. Along the northern edge of those woods, there began to be muzzle flashes. Where it was aimed ... that was another matter. Nothing seemed to be coming toward her position. She called Second Company. "Are you receiving any of that fire?"

"Yes, sir. No result so far. Not clear if it's even aimed fire. I ... Okay, that was a round through the tent. Take cover! Sir, we are now receiving small arms fire at this position."

"Understood, Second. Weapons free on the near woods. Not the woods to the west, understood?"

"Yes, sir."

"Third, this is Command."

"Third Company."

"Weapons free on the farm and trucks remaining on the road. I'll be ordering Armor to move, shortly. Adjust fire to avoid them as they move in. Do not direct fire due south. Toward the border. Understood?"

"Understood."

"Armor."

"Sir!"

"Advance as discussed. South and then west, directing fire on trucks, personnel, and buildings. Remain at least four hundred meters from hostiles until directed otherwise. Understood?"

"Yes, sir. Sir, confirm that this is live fire?"

"Live fire, Lieutenant. Live fire." *Will I ever forget saying that?*

===

There is nothing quite like adrenaline. And making the transition from an apparently successful outcome to a fire fight is a good way to experience its effects. Allen slammed his hand on the headlight switch, blacking the truck out. That was, really, the last reasonable thing he did. He jerked the door open and jumped out. Jimmy reacted in a more reasoned manner. He collapsed his body in on itself and curled up in the foot well. Neither of them saw the other again.

Outside, Allen looked around in desperation. People were running in a range of directions, some back toward their vehicles, some toward the farm buildings, some off into the woods. Since the place was nearly surrounded by woods, that didn't indicate any particular direction. A few of the more aggressive types were trying to give orders, others were clamoring for someone to give them orders. Whatever may have happened to Lou and Doug, they weren't in evidence.

West. That was the primary thing he remembered from his plan. Which way was that? He'd stopped the truck pointing ... what? North? That meant west had to be ... on his left. He turned and ran that way. It happened to be south-west, but he scarcely knew up from down, now, so he ran. *Get into the woods.*

===

"Company, prepare to fire!" The Second Company commander had to admit, later on, that it felt no different issuing that order now than it had many times before in training situations. He had three squads, and each one was as near its theoretical 110 people as the state of recruiting would allow. His First Squad was on line at the right, too close to the west woods for comfort. Third Squad was behind the firing line, in reserve. So he switched from the Company Channel to Second Squad, lined up on his left, off toward Third Company and the Armor. "Second Squad, observe red marker."

"Second Squad, understood."

"All right, Sammy," the Lieutenant said, "Give me a red flare right in front of those people shooting at us."

"Sir!" There was a moment's pause and then a grenade launcher's characteristic *thump* sound. A second and a half after that, a bright red flash lit up the north edge of the finger.

"Second Squad, do you have the marker?"

"Yes, sir!" Beyond the flare, there were more muzzle flashes from the woods. To the Lieutenant's right, someone yelled. Another voice called for a medic.

"Second, five rounds rapid, open fire!"

There were, probably, no more than a dozen or so of the OpFor people scattered along the edge of the woods. It was unlikely that any of them had ever seen ninety-four assault rifles go off at once. The bare ground ahead of them leapt and flung topsoil around. The trees overhead dropped small branches and shards of bark. People shouted, people screamed, people jumped up and ran. A surprisingly small number of them remained where they were, lying awkwardly on the ground. Outgoing fire from the north edge of the finger stopped abruptly. It took another twenty or so seconds for the Second Company Sergeant to stop her people's firing, responding to the Lieutenant's twice-repeated "Cease fire!"

===

The Republic's "armor" consisted of six-wheeled personnel carriers, each with a single twenty-millimeter turret gun and room for twelve soldiers and three crew. The "light armor" were heavy pickup trucks, given some door and side protection and window panels that would stop small arms rounds—for a while. Four personnel carriers and two of those trucks were moving south-west, diagonally down from third Company's position, flanking the OpFor and, in theory, forcing them to withdraw into the woods instead of through the fields.

Another batch of flares went up. "Vehicles," said the Corporal commanding the troop carriers. "Straight ahead." She picked up the radio mic. "Company, Armor. Trucks on the north/south road. Four hundred meters. Do I transmit?"

"Affirmative, Armor. Tell 'em."

Besides weapons, the armor had large speakers. She switched the microphone to the speakers. "Attention. You are here illegally. Drop all weapons. Stand still with arms above your heads. Again, stand still with arms up." The carrier on her right repeated that message. As the third carrier began to say it again, there were muzzle flashes along the wood line ahead. In the flare light, people could be seen running around among a line of civilian vehicles. More flashes. One or two of the trucks began trying to turn around.

"Company, Armor. Incoming small arms fire."

"Understood. Weapons free."

"Gunner, watch for my target mark."

"Sir!" The Corporal swiveled a laser designator back and forth. One of the trucks was in motion, turning toward them. She triggered the laser and centered it on the truck.

"Open fire." The twenty-millimeter gun fired three rounds. "Cease fire." The pickup was burning, and people were running away from it. To the right, the other carrier fired. The light armored vehicles turned broadside and started firing their pivot-mounted automatic weapons. On the road, a parked truck backed into another one, hard, and blocked the way south.

===

Gorsky was standing, leaning on a chair, out in the main area again. "That's live fire, sir," said the Sergeant, pointing at his screen. "If the positions are accurate, Field Branch is shooting... and there's some return fire! From the woods around the farm!"

"Are you hearing this, General?" She was connected with Kydo. Newhouse and Hallstatt were still coordinating support.

"Yes."

I don't like this, Gorsky thought. She moved to look at another monitor, in another cube.

"Major! US forces ... somebody, anyway ... deploying north of the highway!"

"How north? Across the border?" Gorsky turned toward the speaker.

"No. Still south of the border. But somebody's shut down traffic."

"Where?" She took three long steps to the appropriate desk.

"Not clear," the Analyst said. "I'm expanding the view ... nothing's going ... there! Traffic backing up around the rest stop—the travel plaza. They must have blocked it there. Seven klicks west."

"Let's look at the east end! General Kydo, it looks as though the US has shut down traffic on the freeway. Somebody has, anyway."

"Nothing moving west beyond ... Steerling. The big toll place there."

"All right. General, imagery says the US—presumably the US—has closed thirty plus or minus kilometers of the highway, east and west of the incursion site. And there are deployed troops south of the border, across the places where OpFor broke through."

"Understood. I'll reinforce the orders to avoid due south firing. And ... General Hallstatt is back. General, we have firing on both sides. And the US has moved in, apparently. And closed the highway."

===

Allen ran, or tried to run, through the woods south of the farm. At one point, though, a field had been extended slightly into the trees, and he stumbled out into the open. He stopped. To the left, there was just open ground, back toward the road, the trucks, and obvious gunfire. Ahead, there was more open field.

To his right, the woods called to him. Fire from the LAVs snapped overhead. Another round kicked up dirt three meters away. He spun to his right and started to run. A twenty-millimeter projectile near-missed a pickup truck behind him and struck him between the shoulders. He fell, already dying, face first onto the plowed ground.

===

On the western side of the "finger," members of the OpFor were collecting. If they had any shared sense of the situation, it was just that they were receiving effective and continuous fire from the east and north. Some of them had noticed that returning fire seemed to increase the amount of the hostile attention, and there was a growing consensus that withdrawal was the best option. The firing from Second Company had reinforced that idea, and the people coming back from the fingertip were not inspiring confidence in their colleagues; a number of people made the decision to abandon the project. For that group, going south through the woods seemed like a better idea than running west across a wide area of plowed field with no cover. They had not yet discovered that another entire FB Company was deployed across that path, but it still seemed like a bad idea.

There were some dissenting voices. May, for example, the woman who'd been giving Lou a hard time, was not interested in retreat. She was trying to convince the people around her that a rush across the open ground to the north would rout the "damn commie bastards," and that would allow the group to turn east and clean out the rest of the opposition. As her audience continued to slip away to the south, she got more and more angry.

At the same time, Major Franck had moved her command position again, farther south and into shelter around an apparently abandoned shed. This put her and her staff at the north end of First Company's line, stretching south in skirmish order, nearly as far as the border. She was at the edge of a tree line, watching the open areas north and south.

Suddenly, a small group of the opposition ran out of the woods at the end of the finger, going straight north and firing as they went. May had managed to sell her tactical solution to five other people, and they were carrying out a charge across three hundred meters of open field, firing from the hip. Franck was momentarily uncertain. *Is that ... happening?* She immediately concluded that it was, and reached for her field radio.

At that same point, a Sergeant at the front of Second Company's First Squad raised his weapon. Simultaneously, a trooper a meter to his left shrieked and fell over. With that, the whole of the squad's front line opened up. The OpFor attackers dissolved into a small clump of casualties. The wounded trooper gasped once more and died.

===

Jimmy raised his head slowly. He got his eyes up to the lower edge of the truck windows. The small cleared area around the farm seemed to be empty. A burst of firing from the north made him duck back down. He'd been up long enough, though, to see buildings. He'd also seen at least one vehicle on fire. Still staying below the window line, he managed to wriggle across the cab to the driver's side, pop up once more to look around, and then gently open the door. He let it swing open; then, since nothing new happened, he went out slowly, head first like a crawling thing, and lay flat, looking around. Still, there seemed to be no one nearby. He got to his knees, raised up slowly, and peeked over the hood, checking east, then north. He took a long breath, jumped up, and ran west for the barn. Allen hadn't remembered, and Jimmy didn't know that two different manila envelopes in the glove compartment had all of Allen's identification. The body, lying in a plowed field 200 meters or so to the south, was no longer Allen Posten or Rich Baker; it was just a body.

===

Someone misheard something. Major Franck didn't issue any order to First Company. She was absorbed with the situation in front of her. There was still scattered fire coming from the finger of woods, and no obvious way to deal with the clump of bodies in front of Second Company. The Captain in command of First was moving south, on foot, behind his people, checking with them, and — he thought — reinforcing their instructions to remain in place and prevent OpFor from moving west across the open field. Somehow, though, someone heard something else. There were a few incoming shots from the west edge of the finger, and then the center of his position —ninety-four soldiers — jumped up and advanced at a run, out of the woods and across 500 meters of open ground. Field Branch's basic training did not include much in the way of tradition or symbolism, and its people weren't taught to say much of anything in combat except "Yes, sir," and "Drop your weapon." Somehow, though, some deep human behavior emerged, and they started an incoherent cheering as they ran.

In the woods, along the west side of the finger, most of the remaining OpFor saw the troops coming and reacted by running themselves, almost all of them, back down toward the border. Others who were farther from the visible threat still accepted that there was a threat of some kind, and they ran, too. In the dark—the woods weren't really well lit by the parachute flares—direction could be a matter of guesswork, and some came out into the farmyard or into cleared ground below it, but most of those, preferring the woods, turned and went south again.

The exceptions were a handful of slightly steadier people, some of them with a bit of military or police experience. In all, there were four or five of them. Instead of running, they crouched, or ducked behind trees, or lay down, and began to fire. The first casualty was a two-year trooper, hit in the chest. Three or four seconds later, a Corporal was shot through the shoulder.

She dropped her rifle, and bending by instinct to pick it up, was struck again in her neck.

In the west woods, the First Company commander tried to regain control of his people. He ran toward the edge of the woods, trying to reach a point where he could see. He nearly made it, but he caught a foot on a downed branch and fell flat. In the time it took him to get back up and recover his rifle, the remainder of the Company began to advance too.

Franck saw it all happening. She tried to contact First Company, but the Captain was struggling to get his footing, and he was sufficiently deep in a tachypsychic reaction that he wasn't aware of his radio or much of anything else. His entire focus was on regaining control. On her part, Franck was operating on adrenaline, and she leaped from trying to prevent an unintended attack to a decision to reinforce it. She called Second Company and ordered it to advance and occupy the finger. Then she gave Third the order to move *en echelon* south, swinging in behind the armor. When those things didn't start happening instantly, she began to repeat the orders, but stopped. There was an obvious, visible demonstration that Second, at least, got the message.

While Franck was issuing orders to Second and Third, the APCs started shooting up the OpFor trucks. One of the invaders had tried to get his vehicle turned around to go back south, but he started by circling east, and the approaching armor thought it was a threat. They shot the truck to pieces. Then, acting on the assumption that any truck might be a threat, they began shooting at them all, one by one. The third or fourth target was Rich's vehicle. It caught fire. One armor-piercing round missed its intended target and went through the barn. It encouraged Jimmy in his plan of lying flat and surrendering to anyone who asked.

===

"Armor, Command!" Franck waited a moment. "Armor, Command!"

"Armor!"

"Cease fire to the west. Friendlies moving through the woods. Repeat, cease fire!"

"Understood." It took another minute .The guns stopped.

"Armor, Command, move to within sight of the fence breach and illuminate it. With your lights."

"Understood." The APCs turned south. The light vehicles went ahead, taking distance and angle readings to the broken part of the border.

Having prevented — probably — friendly fire through the woods on First Company, she turned back to the issue of First Company and its entry into the finger. She tried again to get the commander on line. On the third try, he acknowledged. *Don't criticize!* she reminded herself. *Analysis later!* "Where are you?" she asked, instead.

"Sir, I'm ... at the edge of the trees! The west side. Trying to regain control!"

"Understood. Take a deep breath." She paused. "Now, try to get your Company stopped short of the woods. I repeat, short of the woods. Second and Third are coming south. Second will be in the trees before you can be. Understood?"

"Yes ... yes, sir."

"When you've got control, continue to act as a barrier to OpFor moving west. North of the border. You're responsible only for hostile movement north of the border. On our side. Understood?

"Yes, sir!"

"And no firing in any vector south. There are ... friendlies ... down there. On the south side of the border." *That's enough*, she thought, *simple, direct instructions. Lessons later*. It did, at least look as though the unordered move east had slowed. First Company was mostly lying down, in the plowed-up soil, and returning whatever fire was still coming out of the trees.

===

"Oh, this is just my favorite thing!"

"Night runs?"

"Nah, I mean gettin' roused out of my bed, firin' up the bird, and blastin' off to who-knows-where. On about twenty minutes' notice." The pilot was fond of complaining, but he secretly enjoyed active work. Too much of his flying around in helicopters was just routine. His craft, a 21HH2 twin rotor transport-and-support ship, was a genuine mule. Troop transport? Sure. Medivac? Yes, sir. Supply? No problem. Blow the hell out of something? As long as it wasn't armored-up beyond the capability of a rifle-caliber mini-gun, happy to oblige.

His objective was some kind of fields-and-forest site, down by the border and about a hundred and thirty kilometers west. Task: evacuate wounded, if any, provide recon and fire support as requested. Three quarters of an hour from the Capital to the site; back to the closest med facility, 30 K away. Refuel up there, too. Anything serious, back to the Capital with 'em. Or Grand Rapids. *Same distance, almost.*

They were getting close, and the ground below was pitch black. Here and there, a farm might have a lit-up space. But usually not. Off growing-season, there wasn't all that much happening.

"Where's the border?" the co-pilot asked.

"What?"

"I-80 runs right along it, down south from here. Almost always some kind of traffic, even now." Now was 0340 hours.

"It's right here," the pilot said, pointing to his map display. "I can see it just fine. We should see flare lights, the orders said. Pretty soon. What's the command code?"

"Let's see ... TP21."

"TP21, HH13. TP 21, this is HH13. Mark landing area."
Nothing happened.

"I see flares ahead. And fire, too. Like vehicles burning. Marking." Symbols appeared on a small screen.

"TP21, this is HH13. Looking for a mark!" Nothing.

"Screw it. Capital Air, HH13."

"HH13, Capital Air."

"I'm using the comm code we were given, but nobody's responding."

"Stand by."

===

"Major, we're hearing a helicopter, but we're not getting any radio response."

"What are we giving them?"

"Sir?"

"What command code? So they know we're the good guys?"

"Oh. Let's see. LF21."

"That sounds right." ... *this is what the brass are for.* She called the command center.

"Yes, Major? This is Hallstatt. General Kydo just stepped away." Kydo was, in fact, in the restroom. When she returned, the SB commander was on the phone to someone at the Capital Air Base.

"No, I don't care. The code is different now! Tell your pilot the code is LF21. Lima Foxtrot two one. Do it!"

"What's happening?"

"We changed the command ID to Live Fire. Air command didn't get the message. They're trying to call Training Program."

"We'd better start keeping track of these little issues. There'll be a lot of Improvement Opportunities."

===

Finally on the ground, in a field surrounded by trees, the helicopter was taking on wounded. They were coming up the back ramp, carried by two soldiers, and attended, usually, by one of the overworked medical department staff. The first one was unconscious, heavily bandaged on her upper body. The solders carried her to the front of the aircraft. The next one was coming in immediately afterward, conscious, and alternately howling with pain and shouting insults. She was severely strapped down. The med techs who'd come in on the flight were taking the first steps, working with both of the patients. The next person came up the ramp, walking.

"What's goin on!" The lead tech was baffled. "What are you doing?!"

"Who, me?" the casualty asked. "I got shot. In my arm."

"Why didn't they you load you first!?"

"Beats me ..." The medical lead was no longer in earshot. She was at the top of ramp, shouting down at the troops.

"How many more?!"

"Uh, two more."

"Save the bad cases for last! That way they come off first!"

"What?"

"Worst last! There's no front doors on this thing! Send the walking wounded up first!"

"The worst hurt go on last?!"

"What did I just say? That's how the hospital'll be cued up. Don't you get any training for this?"

"All right, all right." He turned. "Sammy! Hold that guy. Send up that one. No, that one!"

===

The chaos and gunfire were all up north. Behind him. Lou stopped for a moment, listening. Ahead, behind, left, right ... in any direction, there were other noises, the kind caused by confused humans trying to move quickly through unmanaged North American forest. There were large trees, growing. Large, dead trees, lying on the ground. Young trees, trying to get some light and become large trees. And everywhere, there was brush and briars. At the moment, something with sharp points was clinging to his jeans. He pushed at it with the butt of his rifle, fumbled, and sent a single round flying up into the night sky. Five meters away, one of his colleagues heard the shot and fired a few rounds in some direction. Apparently he hit nothing but trees.

Shit! It was really the only comment to be made, aloud or internally. Lou had spent a few years of his career as the de facto lead in a shipping warehouse. He'd experienced problems, issues, misunderstandings: the inevitable foul-ups that occur, even in six-sigma-capable, engineered processes. The reality of a complete failure — of something going, as he might have said, totally balls-up, was new. He hadn't had time to think about causes, and without that, he had no ideas about blame. *Who* screwed up was just not a useful thing to consider, at the moment. All that mattered was that things *were* screwed up, royally. Plus, he had to think about getting out of this place, back into the US, and ... maybe crawl under a bed, somewhere. And, of course, there was that damn fence to get over.

Doug, Lou's colleague, was in the same state of mind with the exception that he actually did have a plan. He remembered that the point where they'd knocked down the fence was just east of an old farm house. If he could get there, it might be a place to hide. There might even be an opportunity to get to the break-in, slip through, and run back to the woods on the US side. That would be a couple of hundred yards, each way, in the open, but a human tendency toward optimism pushed that fact away.

He kept on moving along the east edge of the finger, skirting the bit of open ground where Rich had died. That gave him a view to the east, still lit by flares, and he saw one of the light armored trucks from Third Brigade driving diagonally down toward the break in the fence. Someone behind him fired at it. The vehicle turned, and its automatic rifle fired back. That was enough for Doug. Neither the house nor the fence break seemed desirable anymore. He turned and ran west, stumbling and deviating from his course. When he ran out of breath, he stopped.

All around, there were the woods. From various directions, there were shots. He owned a compass; it was in his pack, and that had been in his truck. It was now carefully laid out on the ground in front of the old barn. Two troopers from Second Company were on hand, guarding an accumulating collection of evidence.

Doug took another ten steps forward and stopped. Ahead of him there was a narrow gap in the trees. And the gap was bisected, east to west, by the four-meter-high border fence, undamaged and topped with barbed wire.

===

East of the border break, the country road—the route the OpFor had used to approach the break-in site—held a working, inhabited farm. It was on the US side of the border, and the family living there was sheltering in their basement. It was clear, of course, that some kind of armed activity was going on across the road, and they'd done the logical things. They were sheltering, and they were listening to a US radio station in Kendallville, Indiana, and also listening to a device their son had cobbled together, able to receive PR national broadcasts. Neither source had reported much, yet, except that some kind of "incident" was taking place. "Incident, my fanny!" was the comment from the lady of the house. By remaining in that basement, they avoided injury but missed observing a moment in history.

The other light truck from Third Brigade stopped directly at the border, scrupulously training its weapon back north and observing the break-in site. From a space where a few trees stood behind the family's mail box, somebody shouted, "Hey! Soldier!"

"What was that?" said the truck driver. "Somebody say something?"

Again, the person shouted, "PR soldiers! Hey, US Army, here! Let's talk?"

"Get on the radio," said the Corporal in the LAV. "Tell 'em ... tell 'em the US wants to talk!" She opened the door, stepped up on the foot rest, and said, historically, "What?!" It was the first exchange of official communication between the armed forces of the Peninsular Republic and the United States in nearly thirty years.

===

"Go ahead, Franck." Kydo was running out of steam. She wasn't a coffee fan, but this called for it. And they had.

Gorsky used her Brigade supply account to keep the SB cafeteria open and staffed, and Kydo had made similar provision, in her headquarters. Now, the First Division Major was in contact, again.

"General, we have an unusual situation. Third Company—down by the border—is in contact with US forces."

"Contact?! As in ... " The word wouldn't come.

"Not conflict, sir! Not at all! They called across the fence to our light armored units. They want to agree on ... who arrests who."

"I ... don't follow that. What are they asking?"

"We've been arresting OpFor personnel, as we come in contact. They're mostly giving up. The US says it's doing the same thing. And they want to know if we want the ones they have, if we want to turn ours over to them, or ... what."

"Didn't we cover that?" She looked at Hallstatt.

"I think we said we take the ones on our side of the fence, they take the ones that get back over."

"The problem is," Franck explained, "there aren't many getting back over. We've got the broken fence covered, and there's US ... people ... there, too. Anywhere else, they can't get across. They're stuck on our side. Most of them."

"Gorsky, any thoughts?" Hallstatt had fewer and fewer himself.

"We don't have any way of knowing who's who, do we? I mean, who's a leader, who's just a ... follower? Major Franck?"

"Not so far, no. And they're mostly throwing their weapons away. Before they give up."

"Well ... how about pot luck? We do rotary-wing flyovers, over the woods. Saying, "Follow the fence east." And when they get to the break, we take turns. Person one, we take 'em. Person two, the US."

"Are there any houses? Any farms or anything? Where they could hide out?"

"A couple, both on the US side, though. On our side, it's two, almost three kilometers of woods-walking, and a river to get across. Before you get anywhere. It's all nature area."

"All right," Kydo said. "I haven't got a better idea. Major Franck, I assume you intend to go down there? And do the talking?"

"Yes, sir. I ... yes." That hadn't, in fact, occurred to her.

"Fine. Go down there, see who we're talking to, see what they think of the coin-toss idea. And if the answer is anything other than *fine,* we'll get on the phone and take it from there. All right?"

"Yes, sir." She hung up.

There was a silence. Hallstatt looked up. "We're ... negotiating with a foreign power, here. Do you think ER might want to know what's going on?"

The casualties—three Field Branch people so far, plus Colonel Frank, plus at least twelve poor, misguided bastards from the US—appeared in Kydo's mind. And the wounded. Behind them stood Wickham and the person he'd sent down there to instigate this ... thing. "Fuck ER," she said. Of the two people listening, only Hallstatt was shocked.

===

At the truck park—or junk yard—some troops of Second Company were searching vehicles; others were kneeling or lying in a three-sided formation, securing the wooded boundaries of the little farm, north, west, and south. To the east, it was very secure. Third Company was deploying in an angle from north-west to south-east, facing the farm and most of the remaining woods. Every few minutes one of the soldiers around the farm would shout, "Halt!" followed by instructions to whoever was approaching, explaining the mechanics of surrender.

A Sergeant looked around, one more time, checking the scattered buildings. His eyes stopped, dead center on the open barn door. A person was standing in it, hands in the air. "Halt!" the Sergeant said. It took less than a minute to ensure that Jimmy was as harmless as he looked, get him handcuffed, and add him to the group of people waiting for transport out of the active combat area and, presumably, into captivity. It took longer than that for the Sergeant to finish speaking severely to the two troopers who had supposedly cleared the barn already.

===

General Kydo had gone to her office for a US discussion with Newhouse and Otto O'Neill. Hallstatt and Gorsky were holding the fort in their respective conference rooms. They were tired, and neither one wanted to be the first to bring it up. Hallstatt didn't want to appear any less strong and dedicated than his subordinate, and Gorsky simply couldn't imagine anyone else handling her group. She went down that path vaguely, then came up against a disturbing reality. *I've got no succession plan!* "You know, sir," she started, "It seems as though we might be a little thin on the ground."

"Um, define 'we', there."

"Well, I don't think there are many people cleared for ... all the things ... I am."

"I can think of about two, frankly. You and me. And I don't know the tech. At all. And now that you mention it, I don't see anybody who could jump into ... whatever it is I do."

"I can't think of anybody. For either of us."

"I suppose ... O'Neill could at least advise. And General Newhouse. But, still." Gorski realized that he was talking about his job, not hers.

"That's probably something we should talk about. Not now. But some time."

"Yes. Sooner than later, I think. And you know, everybody's in that boat. So is Kydo. And MacDonald is going to have some things to deal with. We brought Matthews into some ... challenges. It turns out."

E rubbed her temples. "I know about some of that. Not much, but some," she said.

"It's just ... procedures. Things that got worked out by one Brigade and not ... cooperatively. Not jointly. Oh, welcome back." Kydo appeared on Gorski's display again.

"That was productive," she said. "We actually got into the discussion, General Newhouse and I. With the US." *ER is going to have a fit*, Gorsky thought. "And they agreed with your idea for taking surrenders. They only had one specification. They asked us to look for a person called James Clark. And return him to them."

"So they did have someone in the group?"

"They said there was a warrant for his arrest. We can believe that or not."

===

In the Coldstream SB post, the Sergeant on duty sent one of his patrol vehicles back down the highway to the border. "Go pick up that video camera. They're not cheap."

===

Tuesday Morning Light

Kristin was up and just out of the shower. She'd had a second text from Gorsky, in the small hours, verifying her continued existence and providing a vague estimate of being home in the morning. As always, Kristin assumed that whatever her partner was up to, in the small hours, would make it into the news. There'd been nothing overnight, and now she brought up her personal machine as she made coffee. At the same moment, the door opened.

"Welcome home," she said. "You look like hell."

"Funny, I feel that way, too. What's that, news?"

"Supposedly. Do you want coffee? Or food?"

"Thanks, no. I've been drinking Army coffee all night, and eating ... something. I just want a shower and a nap."

While the shower was running, Kristin selected the country's mainstream news channel, creatively called NEWS. It came up in the middle of a sentence. "... told reporters this morning that Field Branch troops from Second Division prevented an incursion across our southern border. A press officer from the Army of the Republic had this statement." The view switched to that of a woman in AoR uniform, with a subtitle, *Captain Amy Carol, AoR.*

"Good morning. Around 0200 hours today, a group of civilians forced a border crossing along the Republic's border with Indiana. Because of intelligence received shortly before the incident, units from Field Branch and Security Branch, supported by Health Department medical teams, were able to isolate the intrusion and arrest or eject the persons involved. Gunfire was exchanged, and there will be details on casualties later in the morning. In addition, we can say that the incursion was unofficial, unsanctioned, and until the last minute, unknown, as far as the US Government is concerned. When US authorities detected the incursion, they dispatched military and police assets to their side of the border, and those forces took part in isolating and arresting the perpetrators, in cooperation with our efforts."

Some bad guys busted through the border, out in the country, and the US helped us clean up, Kristin thought. The shower was still running. *I wonder if she's drowned.* As she was going to check, the water turned off. She picked E's bathrobe off the clothes rack, and opened the door just in time to hand it to her. "I heard what the radio had to say. Would you care to comment?"

===

In the US media, the general news was a bit less formal and much less specific. "US forces aid PR in repelling criminal gang!" "Gun-toting right-wingers smash through northern border!" "Breakaway republic fights US breakaway effort!" Slightly more formal sources took a few more minutes to interpret what was being released, and at least one political columnist pointed out that this was the first instance of law enforcement cooperation since Separation.

"The US and the Peninsular Republic, who have for nearly thirty years maintained a stony silence, have finally admitted that there still remain some joint interests and dependencies. I note, however, that what is being called 'cooperation' appears to be at a very tactical level, taking place between members of both countries' Armed Forces, and reaching simple answers to questions such as, for example, who arrests whom? Whether our government and theirs can arrive at agreements on greater issues remains to be seen."

Gorsky, wearing her bathrobe and sipping a glass of juice, frowned. "I really find it conflicting. I mean, when a blue-blood, moderate-conservative, stuffed-shirt like him manages to say something reasonably accurate. And without even knowing it."

"Perhaps there's hope," said Kristin.

===

When Meg got out of bed, she checked her phone. There were two messages, one sent around midnight and one a few minutes ago. The first one indicated that all staff would be expected at the usual starting time. The second one repeated that, and it added a note that the main work area had reverted to its usual lower level of classification. *They turned off the workstations and put away the juicy documents.* Today was her second day as an official, uniformed SB private, first class. The uniforms fit reasonably well, and free adjustments were available in the building's basement supply office. She dressed—

Larry was in the shower — and went out to get the coffee started. Not long after that, she'd heard pretty much the same news stories Gorsky had. When Larry came out of the bedroom, he asked what the status was.

"It doesn't sound pretty," she said. "Turn on the news, if you want. But it seems to be: u*gly things happened, and we stopped them.* From happening. For a while, anyway."

"There was something about the US being involved?"

"That's the funny part. I think they might have helped us."

"There's a first time for everything, I guess." He smiled and she smiled back.

"Last Friday, in fact."

===

After allowing a couple of hours for rest and recuperation, Hallstatt called E. He'd had less rest than she had, and he'd taken his on a cot in the Field Branch HQ. "So, how are you?"

"I'm awake. And my partner is being motherly. I think I'm ready to head back to the office. I can only take a certain amount of mothering."

"Good. Among many other things ... and other people are working on most of those... our people in Second Division are on scene and taking names." He meant that Security Branch personnel had been deployed to the Cub River area, and they'd done the initial arresting, both of healthy and injured OpFor captures. "But there's a thing with our US agreement ... that James Clark guy they wanted?"

"Right. We didn't hear why they wanted him."

"We still don't know that, but by the time we heard about him, we'd already got him, arrested him, and shipped him back here."

"Here?"

"Yeah. It was early enough that the Second Div people hadn't showed up, and the SB presence was from Kléber's Brigade. We flew in ten of 'em, early. To lend a hand. So ... I guess nobody thought about who should get sent where, and why ... they put him and three more on a helo coming back to Capital."

"Ah." It was all she could think of.

"So, what I want to do is get him in a room with you and Klein. See if you can find out ... what's up ... with him. Before we just take him down to the border and give him a push south."

"Yes, sir." *Nice*, she thought. *Klein and I — Klein probably hates SB, right now. And AoR. And me, maybe. And we try to interview ... some guy. Could be worse, though. I could have to fly down there.* "I'll be in the office shortly."

===

"Good morning. We're interrupting normal programming to bring you a feed from Global News

Canada. They're broadcasting a statement from the US Secretary of State. Here's GNC host, David MacLachlan."

"... released this statement a few minutes ago. Here's US Secretary of State, Sharan Yahadi."

"Early this morning, a small group of right-wing terrorists gathered in Indiana, near the border with the Peninsular Republic. Their aims are still unclear, but evidence is building that they intended to create a small holding of some kind in the Peninsular Republic, from which they could stage attacks back into the US. At approximately the same time, security agencies within the US and within the Republic detected this grossly illegal effort and deployed military and law enforcement assets to prevent it. Cooperation between the US and the PR was efficient, and it resulted in the attackers being either repelled from the PR, back into the US, or taken into custody in the PR." She paused.

"Sadly, the attackers opened fire on PR forces, and the PR, acting to defend itself, returned fire. There were casualties on both sides. Because the attackers were demoralized and routed, it was not necessary for US forces to use deadly force. No US military or law enforcement personnel were injured. An agreement was reached, informally, that those apprehended in the US would be subject to US law, and those taken prisoner on the northern side of the border would be handled by the PR's legal system.

"I would like to take this opportunity to highlight the need for cooperation between the two sovereign countries involved in this joint reaction to terrorism. After nearly thirty years of the PR's de facto independence from the US, it is time that we mutually recognize each other as national equals, and the US will be extending proposals to the PR regarding closer relations." The image cut back to the host.

"That was US Secretary of State, Sharan Yahadi, describing a terrorist incident and cooperation between the US and the Peninsular Republic in dealing with it. More importantly, the Secretary seems to have opened the door to informal relations, at least, between the two nations ..."

Gorski had asked for a driver to bring her into the office. She expected to be on her phone, essentially from the moment she stepped out of the house, and she felt that having someone less tired in charge of her commute might lower the chances of it ending up somewhere out in the country in, say, Third Division. So she was able to watch the US statement, having been alerted to it by Hallstatt.

We're going to have keep Wickham and his little adventure very, very dark, she thought. *Like a black hole, dark.*

===

Jeri Klein looked about as sleep-deprived as anybody. She and Gorsky were in Klein's office, in the ER building.

"Thanks for having this over here. Our shop is still ... working. And securing things." Gorsky was functioning, somewhat.

"It's fine. And this guy we're talking to ...? Who is he?"

"That's the objective. We don't know. All we have is that the US people in contact with Second Division asked us to detain him and hand him over. To them. Hallstatt thinks he may have been a US plant. With the OpFor."

"I see why that might be important." She was being much more reserved than usual.

"Doctor Klein, I'm sorry ... I imagine you ... didn't like being ... unconsulted."

"I ... I hate the fact that it came to shooting. I flatter myself that I could have done something about it."

"*You* hate it?"

"I didn't mean you liked it. Or anybody. I just feel ..." Her face changed suddenly. "I feel old. And useless."

It's too early in the morning for this. "You know who's useless? Wickham. The guy he sent down there not only got a bunch of halfwits killed, he's apparently gotten himself killed, too. Or lost. Every one of the casualties is on Wickham. And you're the one here... " she gestured around the office "... who's going to keep it from happening again. I'll help, but you know what needs to be fixed. Let's fix it."

Klein wiped the back of a hand across her face. "You remind me ... of myself. Way back when. When I was a cop, in the US. First, I had cancer. And then I got shot.

And I had to talk to myself that way. Nobody else around. So, okay. I can do that again. Let's fix it."

"All right. But first, let's have a talk with this Jimmy Clark. And you know, I bet we can get Phil Hallstatt interested in fixing things, too. He didn't care for this, either. You can hear it in his voice."

===

Meg and the rest of Third Brigade—those that weren't home, sleeping—were gathered in the freshly-sanitized main room. The Lieutenant, Jack Severin, was there, looking tired. "So ... " he began. "Last night, most of the senior staff worked through an intelligence gathering and analysis exercise, related to an incident in Second Division. You'll have heard, probably, some news coverage, maybe you saw the statement from AoR. Later in the day, we're going to have a kind of mass baptism, in security terms. Everybody is going to be briefed on this, because we don't know what else might come up, and we have to be able ... to ... oh, I don't know, use all our resources. Or something. So, for now, business as usual. But be back from lunch by 1300, if you go out at all. So that we can ...clue you in."

"Sir." Sharon Christopher had her hand up. "Do we have an assessment of the situation now? Are we likely to get calls and assignments prior to being briefed?"

"I hope not. Major Gorski is on duty, now, but she's out of the office. She said she'd be back as soon as she could, at least by 1100. If she isn't and something serious comes up, I'll have to deal with it. I might have to brief some of you on the ... fly ..."

"And, sir," said one of the Security Branch people, "As I was walking in, there was news about the US. Talking about formal relations with us? Did you see that?"

"No. Forgive me if all I can say is *holy shit!*" There was a mildly nervous laugh around the room. "So, maybe that briefing will be ... more interesting, even. But for now, I'll be here. Talk to me if you need to. I'll, um ... be here."

If you can stay awake, Christopher thought. "Thanks, sir. And there's a fresh pot of coffee in the break room."

"Oh, good. Just what I need."

===

Whether or not Hallstatt had prepared the way, it took a surprisingly short time to get Jimmy Clark, Klein, and Gorsky together in a secure conference room. The External Relations department had quite a few of them.

"You've had a rough time," E said, "A flight here, nobody's told you anything. Before we start, are you okay? Do you need anything?"

"Thank you. No."

"All right. My name is Gorsky. I'm in Security Branch. That's our national police. This is Doctor Klein."

"Hello. I'm in the External Relations department. Like a Department of State, essentially."

Gorsky went on. "We're in charge of figuring out what comes next, for you. There are things we can tell you, some of them depend on what you can tell us. The first thing, for sure, is who are you?"

"I'm James Clark. Jimmy."

"Okay. That's who we were told you'd be. And you're here because ...?"

"I was, I guess, arrested. Where the fighting was."

"Actually, you weren't arrested, technically. There are some questions about why you were there. And what happens next. If I had to guess, I'd say there were some other things ... about you. And you might hesitate to talk about them. Is that right?"

Jimmy's eyes were steady. He met Gorsky's full on. "Yes. Until we answer some questions I have."

Klein actually smiled. "Exactly. We thought you'd understand. Would you like to start?"

"All right," he said. "What is my status?"

"Gorsky?" Klein glanced at her.

"Right now, your status is what we refer to as 'witness to a crime.' Since you don't have any kind of ID, let alone a passport, you're also 'national status unknown.' We'd like to see the first one stay the way it is, but we're interested in getting the second one squared away."

"I see."

"Now, *I'll* ask one. Why were you in the barn, down there at the border? When the fighting was over?"

"I hid there. I was hiding in one of the trucks, but that didn't seem very safe."

"I can understand that. How about a slightly broader question? *Why* were you there, technically in the Republic, in a truck that came in from the US?"

"I'll trade answers. Am I the only one receiving this ... kind of attention?"

"You are," Klein said.

"Okay. I came in with the other people. At the last minute. Because it wasn't safe for me to stay ... down there."

"Interesting. If I guessed that you wouldn't be safe, would it be ... because somebody found out something about you?"

"Yes."

Gorski sat back. "I'm going to offer a few more bits of information, without your having to ask. They're things I'd want to know, if I were you." Jimmy nodded. "We discovered ... before you were detained ... that there might be someone with the people who broke in.

Someone who was there clandestinely." She paused. "Someone called Jimmy Clark." Jimmy's eyes were as light blue as Gorsky's were dark, and they didn't react.

"I'm not completely surprised at that."

Klein nodded. "That's what we thought might be the case. Did you know Rich Baker?"

Jimmy did react, slightly. "I heard him talk. I met him once. It was his truck I got a ride in."

"No conversations? No general impression of him?"

"He was the one who ... he seemed to know the most about the Republic."

"Okay. Do you know what happened to him?" Gorski asked the question almost casually. Klein looked very interested.

"No. I don't. He jumped out of the truck. And ran off, I guess. I just got down on the floor and curled up."

"I would have done the same thing." Klein looked over at Gorski. "It's been a long couple of days. Do you want some coffee? Mister Clark?"

"Some water would be nice."

"I'll get some drinks. You and Gorsky carry on."

E leaned forward. "I've been in our armed forces ... they've changed names a few times ... since we separated. From the US." Jimmy nodded. "All that time, I've never seen any kind of combat. I've never fired my sidearm in anger ... as the saying goes. What in hell was it like, being in the middle of all that?"

"I ... didn't like it. I didn't see a lot, but ... it was chaotic. I don't usually like chaos, all that much."

"Nope." E paused, sitting back. "How long have you served?"

He stared at her. A second or two passed. "Eleven years. Plus or minus."

"You talk like a professional. Talking to us, anyway. How was it, dealing with ... we've been calling them OpFor? Opposition Forces. We didn't know any name for them."

"I got used to it. And if they had a name, I never heard it." Klein came back in the door, carrying coffee and a glass of water. She set the water down by Jimmy.

"Don't worry," Gorsky said. "It's just water."

"I'm not concerned. I sense professionality here."

"Mister Clark and I have some shared job experiences," said Gorsky. "Some years of the same ... employment."

"Good. I thought that might be the case. We can shift to getting you out of here and back to the US, then?"

Clark smiled for the first time. "That would be nice. And I should probably say... if you're getting me any documents, my name is actually Marian Delacour. Jimmy was a cover." Gorsky just barely avoided spilling her coffee.

===

In the small notch of open field, two SB troopers were kneeling beside a body.

"Checking back pockets," said one of them, around twenty-four or twenty-five years old, with her braided hair coming down from the back of her duty cap. "Nothing here." She shifted forward. "No watch or ID on the wrists." Her colleague was taking notes on a tablet. "Apparent cause of death ... Lord, I don't know what to call it. Projectile strike, center back, I guess." More typing. "Wearing ... civilian work shirt ... jeans ... black, work-style boots. That's all I can get from this side." She stood up. "Help me roll him over."

"Which way?" The young man was not enjoying this duty.

"Toward me, I guess. I'll take a hand, you take a foot." The body came up from the ground reluctantly. The front was hidden until the last moment. Then it rolled on its own the rest of the way. "Oh, no! That's sick," she said. "Just sick." And that was all the eulogy Allen Posten received.

===

Gorsky made it back into her shop around ten. Some of the routine monitoring work was turning up news from the US and Canada, none of it differing much from the general narrative. "Idiots/patriotic heroes violate border/attack socialist scum, fail miserably/withdraw honorably." E looked at the summaries. *Is freedom of the press really that big a benefit?* Coverage in the PR media was and would remain boringly factual, full of "no further details have been released," and "stay tuned for more information as it becomes available."

She knew, of course, that the area along the Cub River was sealed to anyone except FB, SB, and Medical Department people, and that it would stay that way until cleaned up. She knew that most of the story would be reported, mostly with candor, in the next day or so. It would not name casualties or prisoners among the OpFor. It would name, with appropriate sorrow, the FB fatalities and injured persons. It would carry polite remarks about the US and its involvement in resolving the unpleasantness. And it would lie—by omission, but still lie—about any PR or US involvement in *causing* the problem. The names James Clark, Rich Baker, or James Albert Wickham would *not* appear.

Oh, wait. Wickham and his schemes reminded her. *What about Katherine Connor? She's going to see the news, but ... but what? Will it mean anything to her? Probably not. Ask Klein. And ... we have a new Colonel coming. What's happening there? Nothing. It's only been a day. Hallstatt's been busy. Really busy. What haven't I been doing that I should be? Jack's been as busy as I was. Actually doing things. We need more help in here. ...*

She snapped back. *Down a rat hole.* She got up and went out into the main room. One or two of the older hands nodded at her. *They're as tired as I am.* She walked over to the break area. *I can do this. I can remember how.* She began assembling a new pot of coffee.

Tuesday Slipping Away

An SB staff car pulled up on the Republic side of the Ohio border crossing. "Here we are, sir. I'll just make a call, and there'll be someone to walk you in."

"Thanks," Marian Delacour said. Shortly, two PR non-coms came out. One held the car door, the other took Delacour's arm. "I'll get your bag, sir," said the other. It wasn't a large bag.

They didn't actually enter the building. Instead, they approached a pair of high, solid gates. One officer waved his badge at them, and they swung open, inward. At the far end of a hall, there was daylight.

"All right, sir. Here's your bag. Just walk forward along the hall, and when you come out, you're in the US. Is someone meeting you?"

"Yes."

"All right then." Delacour walked away, down the hall. A figure appeared at the other end and waved. Delacour stepped over the threshold and into sunlight.

"Welcome back," said a younger woman. "I'm Gleason. Northern Midwest Division. I've got your ID and so on." She held out a briefcase.

"Thanks. I hope you've got some clothes for me. Especially a bra. Do you know how long I've been wearing this damn elastic top?"

"I'm not cleared for that information."

===

Hallstatt was somewhat — now, a bit past lunch — less deeply involved in the immediate and tactical aspects of Safety and Comfort. He had, in fact, a spare half hour to talk with MacDonald about details and even some broad-brush aspects of the Colonel's job. He apologized for having left him alone for a day, explaining that the little matter on the news had taken up most of his time. "We'll get you cleared onto that in the next day, before we start the lessons-learned stuff. But one thing I want to bring up is the — anomalous — Third Brigade, here."

"I wondered if that might be a topic."

"Major Gorsky and her people are A, making themselves indispensable and B, really tired right now. If this had been any longer and nastier than it was — and it was nasty — the Intel Brigade would be asleep at their desks. Gorsky briefed the whole group into this particular thing, just for backup, but that's duct tape, if you know what I mean."

"I can see how that wouldn't be ... really safe. Having those people burning out."

"Exactly. So we're going to move up a thing we had in mind, already. We're going to consolidate the Divisional

Intel groups down here, under Gorsky. Those that are any good, anyway. The rest can go back to the Divisions and be cops."

"I have to say, I was never really sure what our group was doing, up in Third."

"And along with that, I'm going to move her and her people — technically, not real estate-wise — out of the Division and have her report to me. Or go on reporting to me. She is now."

"Okay. I'm fine with that. I'm a line cop, basically, and that's what I understand. Honestly, Intel was the area where I'd have had the least to say, to suggest."

"Thanks for understanding. And you're going to have some issues to work out, on your own. Kléber and the new Major, Matthews ... they're finding some ... *complex*, I guess I'd say ... stuff going on. Differences in how one Brigade worked versus the other. Who did what. How long it took to get something assigned. Different kinds of reporting and stats ... just two different shops, really. Between First and Second Brigade. And they both jumped right on your mass mission idea. So as soon as, say, next week, let's get you down here and heads-down with them. And I'll take the sneaky stuff ... Gorsky's team."

The General signed off. He checked a box on his substantial to-do list, and picked his phone back up. He called Otto O'Neill.

===

Gorsky was eating a sandwich of some kind—if you'd asked, she would have had to look at it to tell you what kind. She was wondering whether she could get outside for a few minutes, just to breathe, but her phone went off. *Klein. Maybe about Jimmy ... I mean, Katherine.*

"Hello, this is, I think, Major Gorsky. How can I help?"

"It's Klein. Obviously. I wanted just to ... let you know something." *Oh, oh,* Gorsky thought.

"I just self-reported a security breach. On my part."

"Okay. And?"

"I was going through routine stuff. Yesterday. Printed. All classified. And I dropped a page, you know, down behind my desk."

"Okay."

"Then the phone rang. Wickham's phone. And I had to get it out of my lockbox, and remember its password, and note down what it said." She paused. "And then I had to call you, and be in the call with Hallstatt and Kydo. And talk to O'Neill. And then, I was tired and depressed. And I went home."

"So? I mean instead of doing ... oh, the document."

"I left it on the floor. And I never thought about until I came in. The next day."

"And ...?"

"And then I picked it up and locked it back in my safe."

"I see."

"So, I get a reprimand. But ... it's the first time I've ever done anything like that."

Gorsky shook her head slightly. "I didn't hear that."

"I said ..." E cut her off.

"I didn't hear that. And if anybody asks me, I didn't hear that. And you didn't hear me saying that I didn't hear it, because you didn't tell me any such thing."

"I don't think ... you understand ..."

"Hey, who's the cop here?"

"I see, but between that and just a sense of ... shame. I don't know ..."

"Look, Doctor Klein ..."

"Drop the honorifics. I could call you Major or Doctor or something. But it just wastes breath."

"Fine. But what I was going to say was ... well, look at me. Do I look like somebody named Gorsky?

"I ... suppose not." E's hair was black with a bit of curl. Her eyes were wide and almost black, too. Her nose was long and sharp, and her complexion was a light brown. There was little about her to suggest a Northern European genome.

"I exist because of irresponsible diplomatic people. My father was a US State Department guy. My mother was the daughter of some bigshot in Mauritius." She pointed to her face. "This is my father's nose. Good old Mom and Dad hooked up when he was on the island, then he got posted back to the US, and she came along. I was born in Maryland. That made me a US citizen, and when Mom went home in disgust, I stayed. Dad got a more career-enhancing wife, and I got out of the house as soon as I could."

"I'll be damned. Welcome to the club."

"You too?"

"My parents were black, both. But he and the boys went one way, and Mom and I went the other."

"And here we are. Like John Reed."

"No. It's not ... like that. This isn't 1918."

"We have to do what ... what's *needed*. We don't say 'the Revolution', but 'Safety and Comfort' is the same thing."

"Three of our soldiers died. Four, if you count the guy in command."

"Yeah. And we don't know how many of the idiots made it home. But the plan was to hem them in and starve them into giving up. *Quod erat faciendum*. Unless they fired on our people. But they did. Sadly, they did."

"Foul. Using Latin tags. Don't tell me you've got Greek, too?

"Waiter, two gyros, please."

Klein smiled. "I can't waste any more time beating myself up. Is that the message?"

"I don't get to tell you to do anything. But ... if I have to disagree with you, it's because I *have* to. Because Safety and Comfort. Because, if we like the term or not, we're a Revolution. There's nothing like us. Anywhere."

"Okay, Gorsky. I'll live. With it. With what I have to. Because, as you say, I have to. But I do think I'll see if the NATO2 talks could use a seasoned ... very seasoned ... old hand. And figure out something for the people I have working with you. Maybe just transfer them to SB. Or get the budgets transferred, anyway. Or something. I'm getting tired of *knowing* so damn much." She hung up.

===

Klein took a long breath, held it momentarily, and let it go. *All right, then.* She looked over her list of tasks for the day. *Oh, yes. Katharine Connor.* She got up, checked the floor for documents, and went out to find the other victim of Wickham's folly.

Connor was in the small office she'd been given. She hadn't been given anything to do, beyond writing a what-I-did-with-whom document, so she was carrying out research of her own. When Klein stuck her head in, Connor was looking at a Department of Education site. Klein explained that with Wickham's "retirement," there was no longer a research post available. "However," she said, "the Department owes you, to put it bluntly. Do you have any ideas about what you'd like to do next?"

Connor pointed at her screen. "I've been thinking about that. I had an idea, at one point, about a career in the arts. So I've been looking at degree programs. This one seems as though it might complement my — experience, I guess I could say." The screen was displaying a description of a Master's Degree program in cinema.

"Oh, yes. I can see that. We'd ask you to sign an agreement. You understand, you'd agree not to talk about any of your work here. For your resume, you could call it an internship. And the Department would affirm that, if anyone checked on it. I've been assured that you'll receive compensation and assistance with your living arrangements."

"That would be fine. I think that's really a good path for me." *At least I've had plenty of experience in sex scenes,* she thought.

===

"Major Franck? It's General Kydo." Franck's staff chief was holding out a phone.

"Franck," she said.

"I want to get your people started on a regroup, prior to return to base. More elements of the Second Battalion are on their way from Division Headquarters to take over." Kydo's voice was flat.

"Yes, sir. We're searching west along the border. There are probably no more than three or four more subjects to contact. Shall I call our people in?"

"There's a north/south road that runs down from the approach you took, but farther west. Second Brigade will deploy a Company near its end and move east. They should pick up any remaining OpFor personnel. So, yes, begin withdrawing your people."

"And the ones at the border breach? Cooperating with the US troops?"

"They will be relieved by SB personnel. They'll be on site in a few minutes. You can direct them south to the breach."

"Yes, sir."

"Major, I was instructed by General Newhouse to commend you for taking over unexpectedly and carrying out the mission effectively."

"Thank you, sir." *Effectively? Seemed like a mess, to me.*

===

Lou was tired. He'd been brush busting his way west along the border fence since early in the morning. A few minutes ago, he'd stopped and sat down on a stump. He had no good idea where he was, and only the border fence, twenty feet away, to keep him on course. Now the river had twisted north and he had to cross it or be pushed away from the border.

Then he heard someone coming. From the west. He got up as quietly as he could, meaning to find a large tree to hide behind, but the person stepped into view before he find cover. "Lou?" the person said.

It was Doug. And Doug had a bad assessment of the overall tactical situation. "Troops up there." Pointing off to the west. "Lots of 'em. Pushin' in this way. I had to turn around and come back."

"Well, hell."

"Yeah."

"I suppose we better go back."

"Yeah."

===

In order to avoid unnecessary travel, additional injury, and general inefficiency, Security Branch and the Judicial Authority agreed that wounded members of OpFor would be examined with video links to their hospital rooms. Likewise, their statements and advice would be handled remotely, both with their case Presenters and their Advocates.

"This is a secure examination, carried out remotely since the subject is receiving medical care." the Examiner said, using her formal voice. There was no court reporter. Everything said was imaged and stored automatically. "All records are sealed until unsealed by Council order."

In the Republic, the perception that you'd committed a crime would result in your being detained. You'd be given an Advocate—someone trained in the law and its consequences, but a public employee, not an "attorney" or "lawyer." The private practice of law was actually against the law. Your Advocate would explain your situation, record your statements, and advise you on the likely outcome: either removal of the charges since they seemed to be in error, or an Examination, a kind of trial.

"Examiner," the Presenter said, "the subject is self-identified as Holy Mary the Sword of God. This has been confirmed to be false, per other subjects detained under similar circumstances. Her given name is May Hasfeld. That leads to the first charge, providing a false statement to Security Branch personnel."

In an Examination, the Presenter—a Justice Department Expert on the general kind of crime in question—would present the things you were charged with. For each one, the Examiner—essentially a "Judge"—would agree that, yes, the facts as they appeared in the record did support that charge, or that they require an explanation from the Presenter, or they were in error and did not apply. For each charge, your Advocate would respond, either accepting the charge or debating it.

"All right," said the Examiner. "Advocate?"

"The subject is known to have been present at the events at the Indiana border, referred to in this and other examinations as Disturbance 21876, and she has asserted, in conversation with me, that—and I quote—*I'll call myself any damn thing I please.* I advised her that she has no such right in the Republic, in the context of a legal action. She did not accept that advice."

"All right. Presenter, what else?"

"Illegal border crossing, being in the Republic with no legal basis, importation of firearms, possession of firearms, discharge of firearms with intent to injure or kill, refusal to cooperate with an investigation, and public assertion of metaphysical concepts as literal truth."

"Yes, I see that last one here, in particular. Subject asserted that *The lord god will smot*—what?"

"That's a direct quote, sir. Apparently, she meant *smite*. It goes on in that vein, clearly violating the law against metaphysical proselytizing."

"Subject, do you understand that public preaching is illegal here? Were you advised of that?"

The person on the center screen appeared to be saying something, but it was inaudible. "Turn the subject's sound on." After a few seconds, the Examiner said, "Turn the subject's sound off. I'd add another charge for all that — *narrative* — but she's going to have plenty, as it is."

As far as punishment was concerned, the Republic was unimaginative. The lowest level crimes weren't even brought to an Examination unless you really believed you weren't exceeding the speed limit, or parked illegally, or creating a public nuisance. You paid a fine, and, if you were wise, refrained from doing that particular thing habitually.

Anything else meant fines and, possibly, time in jail. How much time, of course, depended on what you apparently did. Simple things could get you thirty days' imprisonment and "social counseling." The counseling was intended to explain to you, repeatedly, why you were imprisoned and how to keep from having it happen again. That was all local to your place of residence.

"Advocate, anything you'd like to add?"

"Examiner, I'm afraid the best thing we could do in this case would be to confine the subject while she receives further treatment, then make use of the repatriation channel that was agreed with the US. Confining her in the Republic is unlikely to be of benefit to anyone."

For serious things, the imprisonment itself was a mix of traditional jail time, plus a concept born of the Republic's emphasis on Safety and Comfort. For your safety, you were never housed with anyone else. You never had a cell mate. And that kept you from being dangerous to other inmates, contributing to their safety. You ate by yourself, you slept by yourself, you were ... just *by yourself*. No visitors were allowed. You got no mail or messages, except for official topics. You had a view screen, but no control over what it showed. And you were physically *away*; the Republic kept its serious criminals far off in the large, wooded areas of the north, out of sight but never out of mind.

"I have to say that I agree with you. Presenter, agreed?"

"Yes, sir. The subject is seriously injured and is likely to be hospitalized for some time. It would be better for all parties—even her—if she were returned to the US. And, off the record ...?"

"Recording off."

"They have more experience with this sort of person than we do."

Wednesday

"Hold it! Hands up!" There were two SB troopers and a Private First Class on scene, providing security for the border fence repairs. Their attention, quite reasonably, had been on the western edge of the woods, and that was exactly where Lou and Doug appeared. They'd slept in the forest all night, and in the morning began their trek east again. All they had as a guide was the fence, and they followed it, hungry and no longer really concerned with where they ended up. Of course, where they ended up was the edge of the forest, at the base of the finger, right where the whole thing had started. They weren't completely unaware of their situation, physically or legally, and so they'd hidden their rifles in one place, and scattered their remaining ammunition around as they went. Wearily, they raised their hands.

On the US side of the border, there were some minor civilian officials and a reporter, but no military or law enforcement. Doug and Lou got to stand around, cuffed, while the PR Private called back to his Sergeant about having "caught" two more of the "hostiles." It took nearly twenty minutes for one of the light armored vehicles to drive down with an SB Corporal. As that was happening, though, some of the US military people came back, having heard from the civilians that something was up. Nobody present had heard the "one apiece" agreement from the prior day, so this pair of arrests came down to a coin toss. The US Lieutenant won, and they got the remaining two members of the OpFor through the fence just before it was structurally closed.

"Where are we goin'?" Lou asked.

"Fort Wayne. There's some people down there who really want to talk to you."

===

General Newhouse was as rested-looking as the other five people gathered in her secure meeting room, that is to say, not very much so. "This has been a long ... unpleasant ... week. It's been a week, right?"

"Longer, actually," O'Neill confirmed. "And in general, a sad one."

"What are we doing about the casualties? Ours, I mean?"

General Kydo had the answer as she usually did when her Branch was the subject. "We are treating them all in the same manner. All four will receive posthumous decorations, and where there are families, we will make sure they are safe and provided for. Those who want it will be given counseling. All will be added to the list of those who died in the service of the Republic."

"Were any of them without families?"

"Colonel Lamoreaux was a widower, and there is no listed next of kin. He had a dog, and I have offered to adopt it. If it's willing."

"Very well. That's generous of you."

"Not really. It seemed ... reasonable." *I'm not sure I've seen her at a loss for a word*, Hallstatt thought.

"And the wounded?"

"There were relatively few. The weapons used against us are designed for lethal effect, when they actually have the range and accuracy. There were only four others injured by hostile fire, and one of those was hit by a stone kicked up by a projectile itself. They all have good prognoses for recovery."

"Prisoners?"

"Many were turned over to the US. We have seven, one of them injured. They are all being examined and will receive appropriate sentences."

===

Meg was extremely happy. There was, of course, Larry and all that, and now she'd been read in, along with everybody else, on the reality of yesterday's events. There were all kinds of new and fascinating things to learn, code to look at, code to improve, and shortly ... as soon as two colleagues could agree on the requirements ... code to write! And in the jovial mischief category, there was the conversation over breakfast about Larry's parents.

"You know," he'd said, "my folks are old, hard-core lefties. Socialism-with-vocabulary people. Mom is fairly mellow about it all, but Dad still wants ... more words. And more things run by the state."

"There are things not run by the state?" She had her *I'm kidding* face on.

"One or two, still. To hear Dad tell it. He thinks Separation was the best deal we could get, so he lives with it, but he'd still like to see ... I don't actually know what he'd like to see. More nationalization of things, I guess."

"Sure. Just look over there," she'd said. "He ought to be in uniform." Out their window, they could see a man driving by, in an old truck, taking his early crop of cucumbers to market. "And the film school! None of those people can even spell Eisenstein!"

"I'd say Dad was pretty done with Sergei. I remember him being sour about *Alexander Nevsky*. But what I thought we should do for my folks is kind of like the thing with Una? Except live video. We call them ... " He explained his idea. Meg was delighted with it.

"I can hardly wait!"

===

"Now," said Newhouse, "the other thing we want to go over is in Phil's domain, mostly. Phil?"

"So, we have a kind of ... circle of issues, some related to the OpFor situation, some that are just random, and some that are fixes. Fixes for things that haven't worked as well as we thought they would. And the steps I'm going to describe aren't a single, big-bang kind of effort. But they're not tentative, either. They're things I'm sure we want to do, and I think Otto and Doctor Klein are pretty well in agreement, too." Both of those two nodded.

"First of all, I want Major Gorsky to continue reporting to me as a permanent thing. Permanent in the sense that she doesn't report to Colonel MacDonald, when he comes on board. That's thing one." No one seemed surprised, including Gorsky herself.

"The next step is, like that one, something we've been discussing for a while. We want to bring in the Divisional Intel groups, bring them here, and put them in Gorsky's Brigade. She'll be getting the next floor of the building, for that and for additional growth."

"What's there, now?" Newhouse asked.

"Nothing in the way of offices. There's supplies and some hardware up there, but all of that can come downstairs and into the basement or the IT space."

"Okay."

"At the same time, we need to get her Lieutenant, Jack Severin, bumped up to Captain, and get another Lieutenant slot—with or without a person in mind—added on to her compliment. And, especially this: get plans in place to start going a lot farther and deeper in, outside the Republic. In terms of scope and detail." He paused, looking around. No one appeared to object. They'd all heard this much before.

"So that's the near term idea. Call it a timeline from, well, now to five or six months out. To a point where we know how many of the Divisional people will work out."

Newhouse had heard that, too, and agreed with it. "Otto, Klein, Kydo ... any questions?" No one seemed to have any.

"Now ..." Hallstatt said. "Now, we get into futures. Gorsky, this is beyond what we've talked about, but I think it's essential. Once we're sure the Intel model we've built is the right one, I want to split it off from Capital and make it a Division, by itself. With Gorsky heading it up, reporting jointly to General Newhouse and to me."

Gorsky took a deep breath. "I ... see the logic of it," she said.

"And if we're going to follow the regulations, that means you get a Colonel badge. So you can deal with the Division heads on a peer-to-peer basis."

===

"Do we have any kind of ID for this one?" Prisoners, casualties, and deceased OpFor personnel had been flown to the Capital for examination and medical attention. The dead were being checked and identified, where possible, by Medical staff in the Second Division's large central hospital. The person on the table was quite obviously deceased.

"No ID recovered. The list of no-ID deceased is down to three, now." The nurses had been checking people off a *missing* list, as they were examined. The accuracy of the list, of course, depended on statements made by the living prisoners. "Missing" was turning out to be subjective, boiling down to "I ain't seen him."

"We still have Cole, Jason; Burkhart, Donald; and Baker, Richard. All Caucasian males, all alleged to have been present. Not in PR or, so we're told, US custody. And not yet ID'd as deceased." The nurse was looking at a list on screen. An icon appeared. "Update," she said. "Okay ... down to two. Cole has been ID'd on site. Body being sent here."

"So ... *this* person..." he waved at the table "...was Caucasian, male, found north of the border, no ID. There's spine, lung, heart trauma probably from one of the large weapons on the vehicles ... um, no ring or other jewelry, no watch, no phone ... anybody notice tattoos?" No one had. "All right, *unknown*. Cryogenic preservation: five years, DNA samples: permanent. Next." Allen Posten passed out of history.

===

Kydo did look a bit concerned. *But,* she thought, *why not? Other countries do this. Why not ours?*

Newhouse looked at Gorsky. "Does that terrify you, Major? Every promotion I got terrified me, but I got over it. I guess."

"I think I'm more stupefied than terrified, sir. But it hasn't really sunk in yet. I'm ... prepared to accept any orders not actually forbidden by law. But I should point out that I've never stood up a whole new Division. Is there a manual of some kind?"

O'Neill smiled. "I've often encouraged the Army to write one, simply because it would introduce the idea that changes are normal. As far as I know, they have yet to act on it."

"Any time you want to write it, Otto, have a ball." Hallstatt was having his own "Is there a procedure?" problems, internal to Capital Division. There wasn't one, and Kléber and Matthews were having to make it up, issue by issue.

"That, then," he said, "is what I want to do with Intel. There could be more, down the road, but that's what I'm putting on the table, today. The first two points, this group has already agreed on, and Gorsky and I can get 'em rolling. Does anyone have any big problems with the third, the make-it-a-Division idea?"

O'Neill shook his head. Newhouse said, "No. It's logical. And it makes it harder for other groups to go freelancing. No offense, Klein."

"None taken. We've got housecleaning to do in ER, and ... I'm trying to speed that up."

"General Kydo?"

"No. I had to think for a second, but no. No objections." *I will be attending a grim ceremony this week because we didn't understand the problem soon enough.*

"All right. Thank you. You and I, Gorsky, will be a committee of two, to start with, kicking this off. Promoting your Lieutenant should be the first thing. Now, we have one more thing to talk about. General?

"What Phil means is that five of us here are read in on a particular issue, and Major Gorsky isn't. And," she looked at E, "everyone agrees that you need to be, since we seem to be opening ourselves up to the world, just a bit more." Gorsky realized that everyone was looking at her. She nodded. "We pitched this to Councilmember Felix, and he was fine with it," Newhouse added.

O'Neill spoke up. "The last person to be briefed on this was General Kydo, at the point that she assumed formal instead of temporary command of Field Branch. This briefing doesn't happen often enough that traditions have evolved, but I'd like to suggest that she brief you, and that perhaps next time, you'll impart the awesome facts to someone else."

"Are you willing to be read in on a highly secure topic?" Newhouse asked.

This seems like ... a sorority thing, Gorsky thought. *But ... fine.* "Yes, sir."

"All right. General Kydo?"

"The reason that the Republic was able to separate from the United States was that we already possessed a technology, referred to as the Ability, deployed in a belt of geosynchronous satellites. It can disrupt any kind of electrical current, very selectively, regardless of any known kind of shielding. Its range is anywhere on the planet, from a radius of about six kilometers down to a meter. It was two meters when I was briefed, but the precision has been improved since then."

"I'm ... stunned."

Even Kydo smiled. "I was, myself. It has been used, outside of testing, twice. Once to prevent the US Army from invading the Republic ... the event known as The Freeway Fight ... and once again after the Rainbow incident. You were involved in that, of course." E nodded.

"The Ability was used to disrupt a birthday celebration for the then US President, since we had direct knowledge that a clumsy attempt on their part led to the demonstration here."

"I never heard a whisper of that."

Klein, who'd been looking at the table, raised her head. "Nor did anyone else, outside this group. But the US heard the message, and that was enough. Publicly, they blamed a technical flaw in their communications ... and went back to minding their own business."

"This is classified at the highest level, with extensions." Newhouse took a rather primitive-looking phone out of her desk drawer. She tapped something, then slid it over to Gorsky. "Read that, if you would, and then tap the

AGREE block." It took a handful of seconds to create another member of the Ability Cadre.

"Welcome to the party," Hallstatt said. "Outside of genuine crises, you won't see a lot of new information on this. Once a quarter, there's a briefing, held here, same people, on anything new. The fun starts when there *is* a crisis of some kind. And you'll be pulled into that. If the new organization works out the way I hope it will, you'll probably be kicking some of them off."

"Thank, you ... " Gorsky looked around. "Everyone. For trusting me with this. I was on my way to the Freeway Fight, driving a supply truck, when it was ... called off. It's nice, finally, to know why."

===

Hallstatt left the meeting with everyone else, but he ducked into the restroom. After enough time for the others to have made their way into the elevator, he came back out. Newhouse was still in the secure room.

"Okay, the last item," she said. "ER."

"Right, ER. If they're going to ..."

"I know. If they're going to ... talk, let alone anything else, with the US, they need ..."

"Adult supervision."

"Exactly. And I'm sorry, Phil, but you've got to be it. The adult. Felix thinks so. O'Neill thinks so. I think so. And it's going to be tricky."

"Yeah. Investigating a whole department ... secretly."

"Secretly. If you'd known about Wickham, say, when he diverted those jobs from in-house stuff to ... I don't know what we'd call that, what would you have done?"

"Then, I'd have gone, myself, to their headman. Today, I don't know. I'm not sure. I was about to have Kléber, or Gorsky, or Kléber *and* Gorsky look into it, but all this blew up." He waved generally south.

Newhouse nodded. "Now, we start with him. Wickham. Contacts, background ... all that. And then work down. And it's all ... it has to be here, in Capital Division. And you have to be careful about Gorsky's ex-ER people. Remaining loyalties, all that."

"It's not going to be fast."

"Yeah. Neither is the progress with the US, though. We've got time."

"Yeah. And the other thing; Gorsky's ... future. We've got time for that, too."

"Like we said, two years. Maybe sooner. And then it'll be Field Branch, Security Branch, and *Intel* Branch. And — probably — *General* Gorsky."

===

Gorsky walked home. She wanted the thinking time. Somehow the Ability seemed less a shock than the notion of commanding a Division. *Seriously? Me with a green badge? Colonel Gorsky?* She tried to imagine herself, commanding instead of doing. *I like doing things.* That thought led her to another. *So does Kristin. Kristin likes restaurants. And music. And ... parties.* Parties. Social events. The higher you went, the more you did those things. *But, if this is all spooky stuff, maybe there won't be that much. Yes, there will.* Newhouse was often doing social things. She spoke at graduations, congratulated long-serving personnel, addressed Council. Even Kydo did that sort of thing. *Hallstatt goes to art openings with his partner.*

There was a convenient cut-through from the office and government district, off north toward their house. She was still wandering around in her mind, paying little attention to anything else. Someone shouted.

Thirty meters or so ahead, a man was running toward Gorsky. Behind him, someone was yelling. "Stop him! He's got my bag!" *All right, then.*

Gorsky's hand went to her pistol. *You want action? We got action.* "Stop! Right there, sir! Police!"

Ten minutes later, two very surprised Second Brigade troopers found themselves taking a statement from a uniformed SB Major in the uptown area. She was still standing over a man; he was flat on the ground. He wasn't resisting, but he continued muttering things about, "My damn luck!"

"According to the victim," Gorsky indicated an older woman standing by, "He grabbed her bag and started running off with it. I happened be here, and I carried out an arrest. I drew my sidearm, but no shots were fired."

"All right, sir. Do you ... mind ... if I just confirm that your magazine ... is full? And there's no ... residue on the muzzle?"

"Of course not. Procedure, Trooper. Procedure is everything. Go ahead and remove it from the holster." She raised her right arm out of the way. *And I still haven't fired a shot in anger.*

===

"Doctor James Wickham?"

"Yes?"

"You are under arrest, sir. You're charged with fraudulent diversion of national funds."

"That's ridiculous!"

"I don't know anything about that, sir. Turn around and place your hands behind your back."

===

"I have measured out my life in conference," O'Neill said. He was in his office. General Newhouse was in hers, and General Kydo was with her. They'd spent a few minutes making sure they were in agreement on a specific thing having to do with the funerals.

"I can't tell if you're wearing your trousers rolled," said Kydo. There was no trace of a smile; for her to make any kind of witticism was a rare thing. *I wonder if that's a stress response,* O'Neill thought. *Or is she perhaps getting a bit tired of it all? Like all of us?*

"We are certainly deep enough in this that I might have to. It's a genuinely vexed question. We could include others than ourselves in the discussion, but my perception is that we should agree on it, here, and then attempt to get Council and External Relations to agree with us."

"Without delaying the ceremonies." Kydo was still solemn.

"Right," Newhouse said. "We owe everyone that. So, then, what do we think? Do we want a silent, respectful United States Army officer at the funeral?"

"And will we provide the press with prior notice? Explain that person's ... utterly, unquestionably neutral significance? Say what the US has said, that they feel they owe it to our people, killed by US banditti? And he or she will only appear if we wish?" O'Neill was as grim as anyone had seen him.

"I think we do. I think it makes a difference." Kydo's face betrayed just a ghost of emotion. "This isn't something for analysis. It's ... human."

Will wonders never cease? Newhouse passed a hand under her eye. "I agree. I think the Army can ... *lead* ... on something like this. They were our people."

===

Thursday

Meg and Larry had just finished a call to Karen Mather. Meg remembered that she'd never told Karen *who* she was planning to seduce, and since Karen knew both parties, she deserved a status report. It was an amusing call; Karen appeared to be concerned at first, then admitted to having been kidding. "You two have fun," she concluded.

"So," Meg said, "What are we going to see tonight?"

"A band. Some friends of mine play, sort of, at The Fish Fry." Larry was reaching a point of confidence in the relationship with Meg that suggested introducing her to his acquaintances. The Fish Fry was a bar, technically, on the city's east side. It had only a beer/wine license, and no food at all. "Bring your own damn food" was its policy in that area.

"Lovely." She meant it. Her circle of friends was limited, the majority being—as she was now starting to think—"other cops." She'd been in uniform for two working days, so far, but she was buying into the image. It widened her circle, even if she had to salute a substantial number of its members. "What do they play?"

"It's, um, strange stuff. They call themselves The Remains of Nothing. It's sort of nihilist folk rock. It was a movie, once, I guess."

"Really? Do they have any recordings?"

"They're working on an album. They want to call it *Nothing Remains*."

===

Gorsky was up, in her robe, making coffee while her partner was getting dressed. On days where there was something happening, reins-of-power-wise, in the Department of Education, Kristin's getting-dressed behavior typically called for music. Someone at PRBroadcasting was spinning early Grateful Dead. The music shut off, and Kristin came out, wearing one of her more severe suits. "I have a question for you," she said.

"Yes?"

"What did actually happen to sweet Jane?"

"Lost her sparkle, I guess. That's what I heard."

"Better than having it removed, I suppose."

When they parted and went off to their respective concentrations of ruthless state authority — offices, as some would say — each one spent the brief travel time pushing away the tactical and considering the existential. Gorsky was thinking over an insight, not one especially welcome, but hard to push aside. *It's my father. I'm ... competing with him. Took my time about it, but I'm turning into him. Authority. Rank. But ... oh, right ... not exploitation!*

It would have been hard to define a less exploitive relationship than hers. Kristin had admitted, at the outset, that *she'd* been stalking E. True, they'd lived for a while in a little house in the big woods—in the literal, not the Laura Ingalls Wilder sense—but that was because they both worked up there in the northland, dodging bears and discouraging smaller wildlife from dropping in unannounced. *We chose that. Jointly. I'm not sure my mother chose anything about her adulthood. Sex, marriage, parenthood ... any of it. But ...* another thought. *Did I choose any of this?* By "this" she meant the cascading string of promotions and admissions into circles of power.

The tram was getting close to her stop. *Would I have said no? To any of it? Would I have tried to get promoted? Over and over? Or into a relationship with Kristin? She found me, not the other way around.*

She stood up when the vehicle stopped, and, with several other people, got off. She nodded to a journalist she knew, smiled at and returned the salutes of two people in her group, and went into the building. *Oh, well. Carpe diem, or something. Carpe difficultates ... seize the day's trouble.*

Kristin, on the other hand, walking north toward the Department of Education and her own office, was less inwardly directed, thinking just briefly about her relationships, the one she'd ended, then coming into the PR and finally getting within partnering distance of Gorsky. Her fears were centered on stagnation, loss of humor and humility, and limits on spontaneous ... *horsing around. Fun.* She was, of course, moving up the ladder in the DoE, managing change and when possible, changing management. And, as it often did, her mind came up with a variation on an old theme. *What was it, now? Some are born to greatness, some have it thrust upon them ... some stumble blindly over it in the closet, looking for something else. Oh, it's greatness. Who put that there?*

She walked the last three or four steps to the staff door, waved her badge at it, and it opened. As she went in, she realized why so much of her conversation with E was humor and outright sarcasm. Neither one of them was willing to give in an inch to fear, any more than either of them would have remembered David Crosby or 'Almost Cut My Hair.'

===

The day ended and the evening arrived. There'd been a glass or two of wine. Gorsky looked at Kristin's eyes. "Are you happy with ... this?" She made a gesture taking in the dining room, Kristin, and by extension, their lives.

"Yes. I am. Extremely happy."

"I am, too. Certainly. With this. I'm ... a little uncertain about the rest of it."

"I know. I heard about the casualties, ours and the ... crazy people. And there's probably going to be a civil war in the US. That's not *all* there is, though. Out there." She waved a hand at the window."

"Right. Keep telling me that." E held out her glass. *The job is not more important than us.*

===

"I ... am freaking exhausted." Lena Kléber and her partner were on their couch. "I don't know about you, my dear, but I need sustenance. And I don't think I can stand up long enough to cobble it together."

"That's pronounced with a 'th' at the beginning. And I've dealt with it."

"How can I ever thank you?"

He put his hand on hers. "That's taken care of. Long ago."

===

The Art Department's gallery was a usual venue for evening social events, show openings, and all the audible and visual exposition that an art teaching organization required to sustain its need for socialization.

"Half of these people wouldn't come if it weren't for the snacks." Doctor Jerry Villars was gently moving his partner, Phil Hallstatt, toward the hors d'oeuvres and the always-hungry graduate students gathered around them.

"Ayesha," he said, "This is my partner, Phil. This is Ayesha Williams. She paints beautifully." Hallstatt was polite and as charming as he could manage to be, since every young person he looked at reminded him of those being given military funerals the next day.

===

Posh. Definitely an improvement. Matthews looked around. The apartment was not really luxurious by Capital standards, but it beat the hell out of living in Seventh Division's barracks. Or in Seventh Division, period. She looked lovingly along a shelf of her books, just now unpacked. She lingered at Bernard Fall's *Street Without Joy* and a ragged copy of *Hell in a Very Small Place*.

I got the job. I got a place to live. There's a grocery store two blocks away. What else could I want? The old thing about a woman needing a man like a fish needs a bicycle came to mind. *I could get a bicycle.*

===

The MacDonald family were packing. The new Colonel and his partner had packed up several times in his career, and this was the second time for his daughter. She had been and continued to be excited about moving to the Capital. "Dad, does our house have a view of the government?" He smiled.

"The government isn't really one thing, in the city. It's ... kind of part of it, snuggled in and around things. And now that I think of it, it works the other way, too. The city sort of *is* the government. Things start there, most of the time. Sometimes they start other places, but ... " Recent events came to mind. "... it's better if they start *there*."

===

Jeri Klein was at home, a little earlier than usual. There were already rumors around the Department. *Bad things had happened. Investigations were starting. This person or that person might have to retire ...*

"The hell with it," she said, aloud. She found some leftovers, got them warming up, and poured herself an ounce of bourbon.

===

"Hello, Larry. What's up?"

"Hello, Mother. Is Dad handy?"

"I can call him. Jack! Larry's on the phone." There was a minute's pause.

"All right, all right. What's up?"

Larry stepped slightly to the side. "Mom, Dad, I'd like to introduce you to a uniformed agent of socialist repression." Meg stepped into view. "And the love of my life." Meg was wearing her SB gear.

"Hello, I'm Meg. I'm afraid I've recruited your son into a life of doctrinaire monogamous conformity."

"She started it!"

His father arched an eyebrow and glanced at his wife. "These kids, today," he said.

===

In George Pickett's bedroom, the window was open slightly. There was a breeze coming in off the lake and blowing across the bed.

"At least ... " George said "... we have the lake ... as a border ... from the idiots ..."

Ciela's eyes were closed. "Yes ... yes ... we do ... and we should ... just ... just ... just! Wish ... them ... away!"

===

277

Outside The Lake House, a large dog curled up at the front door and went to sleep.

About the Author

 Joseph McConnell is, in his seventy-first year, a board-certified cranky old guy. This is his eighth novel. Others include:

About the Peninsular republic:

- *Dog Island*
- *The Stars Came Otherwise*

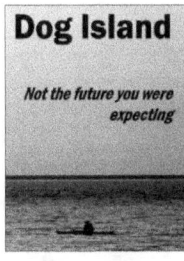 

About crime and punishment in the City of Ann Arbor:

- *Many Believable Lies*
- *Clash by Night*
- *The Least Weasel*
- *A Lair for the Wolves*
- *Driven by the Trades*

Upcoming projects include, perhaps, another look at the Peninsular Republic and its government.